I0747793

Other books by Deirdre Hutchins

The Paranormal Investigators League series

PIL #1 Voodoo in Savannah

PIL #2 A Hanging in Tucson

PIL #3 Suicide on Sunset

PIL #4 The Legend of Providence

PIL #5 Darkness in Denver

PIL Prequel: The Origin Story

The Dark Prophecy trilogy

1: Resurrection of the Vampire

2: Vengeance of the Damned

3: Deliverance from the Prophecy

These are all available from the San Joaquin Valley Press.

Visit us at www.sanjoaquinvalleypress.com

The Dark Prophecy

Book 3: Deliverance from the Prophecy

A Novel about Vampires and Witches

By Deirdre Hutchins

San Joaquin Valley Press
Fresno, California

The Dark Prophecy is published by
San Joaquin Valley Press
P.O. Box 9485
Fresno, CA 93792
www.sanjoaquinvalleypress.com

Cover design by Andria Davis Kaye

ISBN 978-1-7378061-3-4

1

"At least teleport us to the Canadian border," Isabelle pleaded as a twig crunched beneath her foot. The sun would sneak through branches every now and again, but for the most part they were hidden under a ceiling of branches, foliage and thicket. The path they followed was a well-worn trail winding through the mountains, wide enough for one person, with Camilla a few steps ahead of Isabelle.

"Yes, but I already told you, I need one more ingredient." Camilla shoved a branch out of her way and kept hiking and talking without turning to look at Isabelle. "It isn't like I had time to carefully pack all my potions before we left on this rebellious journey."

"No one forced you to come," Isabelle sneered, her anger, exhaustion and hunger allowing her fangs to slip out to where they rested on her lips. They had long since ditched the motorcycle that Isabelle had taken from the compound, Camilla riding on the back with her arms around Isabelle.

The decision to go had been spontaneous to say the least. Camilla wasn't even completely sure why she'd agreed to come. Isabelle had never been her biggest fan.

And yet the journey was the easiest part of this whole excursion.

When they arrived in Bianca's cave, the real work would begin. Camilla had spent a decent enough time around vampires, both as friend and foe, that she felt somewhat aware of what lay ahead. Yet at the same time, even the fiercest of the vampires on Shane's council had been scared of Bianca. Camilla truly didn't know what to expect, but she imagined a wrinkled old crone with hairs coming out of random pores.

Then again, that was the witch in every movie she'd ever seen, not vampires. In the movies, the old evil vampires were always men. The females were there as seductresses. Was Bianca actually a beautiful siren, luring men to their death with some vampiric call, having them lock their gazes on her beauty and then eating them alive?

Camilla shook her head to rid herself of the thought. Theresa had always accused Camilla of being like a siren, and she couldn't untwist the accusation from her own perception of self. And Camilla wasn't scary. Bianca was. No, she had to be ugly.

Evil was ugly.

"What do you imagine Bianca looks like?" Camilla asked, thinking out loud as she found her footing on a particularly uneven area of ground. They had just begun a slight incline and her thighs already burned with exhaustion. Isabelle wouldn't get tired as long as she fed, but Camilla would.

"Don't care," Isabelle replied. She had always been mission-driven and her eye was on the prize. Whether Bianca was a beauty or a nightmare, Isabelle would do what had to be done to get the information needed. Her black boots were much more conducive to hiking than Camilla's tennis shoes, and she stepped purposefully on a fallen branch, enjoying the snap of the wood and the crunch beneath her boot. Isabelle barely resisted the urge to twist her foot and rub the broken branch in the dirt, just to dominate it.

"But don't you wonder why everyone was so scared? Shouldn't we understand our enemy before we attack?" Camilla asked over her shoulder, lifting a low-hanging branch out of the way.

"Let me tell you what I've learned in my undead life," Isabelle responded, eyes as hard as coal. "Vampires are actually big babies. She's probably a total bitch, but now her reputation is larger than she is and it's morphed into the legend of some evil soul-destroying ancient monster. Either way, bitches and monsters don't scare me."

Camilla nodded. She knew it was true. Isabelle was pumped, excited to have purpose. And Camilla had yet to see the creature that scared Isabelle.

Suddenly, a crunch in the distance off to their right froze Camilla in her tracks. Isabelle put a hand on

Camilla's shoulder to let her know she'd heard it too. The trees were thick and there was no civilization for miles. There could be anything lurking, watching them.

Isabelle listened and her hearing was much crisper than Camilla's.

"Stay here," Isabelle commanded with a whisper in Camilla's ear.

Camilla barely had time to register the words before Isabelle sped off so fast there was only a blurry trail where she'd once been. Camilla knew herself to be a smart, capable witch, but alone in the woods like this she felt vulnerable.

She couldn't shake the feeling that something was terribly wrong.

She strained into the distance, trying to see what had made the noise and trying to catch a glimpse of Isabelle, but it was no use. All she saw was forest. And every heartbeat with no sight or sound felt like an eternity. Where was Isabelle? She couldn't believe anything but that Isabelle would be the victor in any fight, but the not knowing was grating on her nerves.

Another crunch alerted her and she turned quickly toward the noise, her heart hammering in her chest. Another crunch. Footsteps. Something was coming slowly toward her. Camilla got her hand at the ready, prepared to use witchcraft to defend herself.

A branch in the distance moved and a figure became clear.

Camilla exhaled as Isabelle's features came into view. The front of her shirt was covered in blood and she gnawed on what looked like a giant turkey leg. When she got close enough, she smiled at Camilla and her teeth were covered in blood.

"It's no Caucasian male, but it keeps me from eating you." Isabelle raised an eyebrow and then marched past Camilla to sit on a log that was nestled between the trees.

"What was it?" Camilla pulled her brown hair over one shoulder and sat on the log not too near Isabelle. She didn't want to get covered in blood.

"A boar, believe it or not." Isabelle licked the

bone and Camilla looked away.

"Why me?" Camilla asked quietly, changing the subject suddenly. Once again her thoughts were just popping out of her mouth. "Why did you invite me to come with you?"

Instead of responding right away, Isabelle slowly licked each of her bloody fingers, smiling through bloody teeth. "Cuz I needed a witch and I knew you'd say yes."

Camilla sighed and pulled out a protein bar. Her stomach was a bit tight from watching Isabelle delight in her bloody snack, but at the same time she knew she needed to eat too. She would need energy for hiking, casting spells, and whatever lay ahead with Bianca the evil vampire. She unwrapped the packaging partway, enough to not actually uncover the protein bar but have enough peeking through that she could take a bite. It was pasty and tasteless in her mouth. She thought about using magic to make it taste more appetizing, but then decided it wasn't worth the effort.

"I'd do it too if I were you," Isabelle stated. She

was still stained in blood on her mouth, her shirt and her fingers, but she didn't seem to notice or care.

Camilla took another bite and then chewed on one side of her mouth before asking, "Do what?"

"Face an evil monster like Bianca to protect Shane." Isabelle tucked her feet underneath her on the log. It didn't look very comfortable to Camilla, but she was enjoying the respite. The air was crisp up here in the mountains and they didn't have direct sunlight to drain them. And still, she was the human in this duo. She just needed breaks that Isabelle didn't. "I'm doing it for me. My sense of adventure and the added bonus of saving all the vampires," Isabelle continued.

"I know," Camilla said, looking straight at Isabelle. Even though she and Isabelle weren't always the best of friends, she understood her. She sat in silence for a moment before explaining. "I don't know anything about Bianca. She isn't known in witch lore. And while it is true I don't want any harm to come to Shane, my gut tells me Shane is more powerful than she is." Camilla looked down at a rock near her foot.

She stared at the rock as she kicked it and it flew into the trees. "So it isn't just that."

Isabelle stood with a blood-stained smile. "Ah, I see. We're both far more alike than I thought."

Camilla stood to match Isabelle, thankful that Isabelle hadn't made her say it out loud. She wanted her day of glory no less than Isabelle did. She wanted the ultimate test of her powers. She wanted to face a powerful adversary and walk away the victor. And, in doing so, she was protecting Shane, so it was the perfect plan for everyone. When Isabelle had approached her about heading out on their own, the thoughts hadn't been fully formed yet, but in a split second that inner desire was driving decisions.

"I never really told you how badass you were that day," Isabelle said as they resumed their hike. "With Theresa. You just ended her."

Camilla showed no emotion as she explained, "I just used everything she ever taught me about being a witch."

Isabelle was still smiling. "That must've been

an ironic kick in the boobs for that bitch." Camilla *almost* laughed at that. Almost. She huffed a tiny puff of air that might have been close to a chuckle. This encouraged Isabelle. "She thought she was going to use you to bring down the vampires, but twist! You tricked her into becoming four hundred years old in an instant. Take that you wicked old witch!"

"Shane isn't a vampire to me," Camilla explained. She was about to tell Isabelle how she knew that Shane was so much better than Theresa. That despite being a blood-sucking vampire, he had more good in his heart than she ever had. And witches aren't necessarily bad. Theresa was. But before she could say anything else, her eye went straight to the tree line. "I can't believe it."

"What?" Isabelle was on high alert as she watched Camilla beeline for a spot near the trees. She used her keen sense of sight and her powerful sense of hearing. But everything seemed calm and peaceful. She saw Camilla kneel on the ground and pluck something from the earth.

"Do you know what this is?" Camilla was smiling, a rare sight. She held her hand up for Isabelle to see a tall stem with purple flowers jutting out at many points along the plant. It was pretty, if you were into that sort of thing.

"How the hell should I know what that is?" Isabelle put her hands on her hips and cocked her head toward the side in a very sarcastic way.

Camilla stood up and walked slowly back toward Isabelle. The look on her face was that of a teacher with her pupil who has been slow to learn. "This, my vampire friend, is thistlewaite."

"Sorry. Left my botanic dictionary at home. Why do I give a shit?"

Camilla put the flower right under Isabelle's face. "Because *this* is the ingredient I needed to transport us to Canada."

Both girls smiled at that. They could be facing Bianca down by nightfall.

2

"We need a witch and a locator spell," Shane said, an order to Luke. Luke nodded and turned to follow the instruction but stopped when he saw Elias walking toward them with Emily by his side.

"Emily's awake," Elias announced, as if that announcement were necessary. They all gathered in the center of the garage. A strip of sunlight was sneaking in through a small window, but they were easily able to avoid it.

"Do you know how to do a locator spell?" Shane asked Emily.

Her large eye roll premeditated her answer. "I

may be a new witch but I'm not a baby." She held her hand out, palm up. "Give me something of Camilla's or Isabelle's."

Shane reached in his pocket and pulled out Camilla's necklace, the one she always wore. He dropped it in Emily's hand without explanation.

"You were just holding on to this for safe keeping?" Emily raised an eyebrow questioningly.

"Considering she left it on the counter where she knew I'd see it, I am very confident that Camilla wanted me to do this." Shane folded his arms across his chest.

Luke shook his head. "Then why did they run off like that? They could have come to us and we could have all gone together."

"You know how impulsive Isabelle is." Elias tucked a loose strand of long black hair behind his ear.

"And Camilla wasn't going to let Isabelle go alone," Shane added, although he sensed there was more to the story, but the detail kept escaping every time he tried to grab onto it. *Had Camilla used magic to block him from being able to sense her thoughts and emotions?*

"Quiet, please. I need to concentrate," Emily instructed, and like good little boys they all stopped talking, eyes focused on Emily who was focused on the necklace. She sprinkled some herbs on top of the necklace, flakes falling all around her hand. "Fire, please. And just burn the herbs."

Shane smirked but complied, using the tip of his pointer finger to send a small flame to the herbs sprinkled across her hand. It burned for a couple seconds before she said, "Ouch," and dropped the contents from her hand, shaking her hand at the wrist. "That was hot." She looked up at Shane, who smiled in return. He knew what she knew.

Luke looked between them. "What? Some of us aren't psychics."

"I got them," Emily smiled widely at Luke.

"So where are we going?" Elias asked the obvious question.

"Grab cloaks, my vampire friends," Shane

answered, bending down and picking up Camilla's necklace before placing a hand firmly on Luke's shoulder. "We're heading to Canada."

"Canada? The last time I was in Canada I was chased by an angry mob," Luke responded. His handsome face was contorted in a way that expressed disappointment in their final destination.

"They found out you were a vampire?" Emily asked, a worried expression across her young face.

"No, I slept with the mayor's sister," Luke answered. "It's a story for another time." He waved his hand in front of him, as if that made the story disappear.

Ignoring Luke and his antics, Shane asked Emily, "Can you transport the three of us to where they are?"

"Yes, but let me get you something first." Emily ran back inside the house, leaving the three vampires standing in the garage watching her go and wondering what she was getting.

Shane turned to his two closest friends and

allies. "We don't know what to expect with Bianca. I don't blame either of you if you decide to stay behind."

Elias beat his fist to his chest. "I'm a warrior and have been for centuries. I will not evade a mission as important as this."

"Yeah, and I'm not letting you and two girls go face the scariest vampire ever to walk the earth while I sit here eating bon-bons," Luke smirked. "Even if one of those girls is Isabelle, who may one day be scarier than Bianca herself."

Shane nodded. Luke had a point. "I want to catch Camilla and Isabelle before they face Bianca so we can head in there with a plan. Somehow, I know that Bianca can sense us coming."

"You don't think we can just walk in and say 'Bianca, we need to talk'?" Luke smirked. Shane looked at him dubiously. Luke shrugged. "Didn't think so."

"Okay." Emily walked back into the garage with two cloaks and a tall glass of murky liquid. "Each of you drink some of this."

"As delicious as it looks..." Luke backed away

from the swirling contents.

"Relax," Shane instructed. "It's the potion the witches drink to rejuvenate." He grabbed the glass from Emily and took a swig. He wiped his mouth with the back of his hand and winced with a face of pure disgust.

Elias grabbed the glass from Shane and followed his leader, disgusted face and all.

"You know, your faces aren't exactly portraying a glowing endorsement," Luke said as he hesitatingly grabbed the glass from Elias.

Shane coughed and sputtered, "It tastes like dirty feet."

Emily shrugged. "I didn't have time to glamour the taste. But it will protect you." She looked up at Luke with a scolding stare.

"All right, all right. Dirty feet, here I come." Luke took a moment to gather his fortitude and then gulped the remaining contents in one swallow. His handsome face contorted into a squinting sour-pucker. "Oh, gross. I was thinking dirty feet, but that was more like rotten butthole."

"Vampires can be such babies." Emily shook her head and handed Elias and Luke their black witch's cloaks.

Shane had composed himself while Elias and Luke were still getting over the taste, although Elias hid it far better than Luke. Every bit the warrior, he didn't let dramatics overtake him. Just puckered lips and a disgusted face were the only clues he hadn't liked the drink, not the coughing and complaining of Luke.

"Thank you, Emily." Shane put his hands on each of Emily's shoulders. "I'm glad we're no longer enemies."

Emily surprised Shane by wrapping her arms around his waist. "Me too. Thank you for taking care of my sister."

Shane squeezed her. "You and Kara are family now. And that's why I will end the Dark Prophecy." His voice was steady, confident. Everything about Shane was solid stability.

It made her miss her dad.

Emily pulled away and swallowed the embarrassment that followed the tears welling in her eyes. "I'm not sure I believe that you can change what's meant to be, but I know if anyone has a chance, it's you."

"If it hasn't happened, it can be stopped." Shane tapped her chin with his pointer finger, something an older brother would do, and she felt secure again. His presence was definitely comforting. She could see why the vampires all looked up to him.

Emily stepped back. "Come back safely."

Silently, Shane nodded. On his left, stood Elias, tall and fierce, like a Native American spirit warrior, his black hair flowing on his shoulders, his chin held high. Luke, on his right, handsome as a movie star with a smirk on his face even as he prepared to face an unimaginable foe.

"Do me a favor? Give Julianna a kiss for me," Luke said.

Emily just nodded and, with a deep breath,

swirled her arm around the vampires and used her magic to send them to the Canadian border, to the exact spot where Camilla had transported herself and Isabelle not too long before.

3

"The cave is up this mountain," Camilla informed Isabelle, who was following closely behind.

"Finally," Isabelle muttered. If she was nervous at all about facing Bianca, it wasn't showing. Camilla was nervous, but she hoped beyond all hope that her plan would work.

The mountain wasn't particularly steep, but Camilla moved carefully and methodically, placing her feet in just the right spot as she went. If Isabelle suspected anything, it didn't show. She followed Camilla in careful steps up the hill. Step by step, they were making their way to the location of the vampire who would soon seal their fate, either stopping the prophecy or slaughtering them for entering her lair.

The early afternoon sun was piercing, with not a cloud in the sky. The magic Camilla had surrounded Isabelle with seemed to be doing the trick. At least, she wasn't howling in pain. They just had this one last hill to climb and she'd be safe from the sun's rays. But then she'd be facing Bianca, and Camilla wasn't sure yet which nemesis was worse.

She hoped beyond hope that the rumors were exaggerated. Well she knew that reputations could become larger than life; she had escaped her own reputation when she joined Theresa.

So she knew the stories about Bianca. She had listened carefully as the vampires talked. If she had learned anything from her years as Theresa's underling, it was to quietly soak everything in and carefully devise a plan. But never let your cards show. Theresa had been a master at it until the very end when she fell apart. Camilla felt that this was a skill she also performed well. And she had to use it to her advantage here.

The small shrubbery crunched beneath her

foot even though she tried to step around it. But as she silently hoped to herself that the sound wasn't so loud as to alert Bianca, she felt a magical connection to Shane. Handsome, glorious, powerful Shane.

He was transporting and their time was up. She froze, looking back at Isabelle. "Shit. We gotta move *now.*"

Isabelle nodded, her lips tightly pierced, her eyes fierce. She was mentally alert and ready for anything. All her life she had been fighting just for the sake of fighting. For territory, for love, for revenge. This was her chance to fight to save vampires and she knew she would take it, even if it cost her her life. She assumed Camilla was worried about the loud step she had taken and knew they had to hurry if they still wanted some sort of element of surprise on their side.

Isabelle kicked in a bit of vampire speed and passed Camilla on the climb up the mountain. Camilla moved as fast as her human legs could take her and arrived not too long behind Isabelle. The mouth of the cave stood looming before them. They exchanged a look, hesitating. The dark cave was an ominous sight. It dared them to enter with an evil bidding, as if to enter the darkness was to be swallowed whole and never to be seen again.

Isabelle straightened herself and said, "I go first."

Camilla didn't argue with Isabelle as the feisty vampire stepped out of the sunlight and into the shadows of the cave. Camilla glanced over her shoulder, hoping she had enough of a head start over Shane. She knew he would follow her, just as she'd planned.

Stepping into the darkness, the first thing Camilla noticed was the cold. It wrapped them in an icy embrace. There was nothing inviting about Bianca's home. It was dark, cold and filled with foreboding. Up ahead she heard the steady drip, drip, of water, but saw only darkness. Knowing Isabelle could see in the dark with vampire eyes, Camilla clutched the back of her shirt to allow Isabelle to guide her. Camilla fumbled in her pocket for a small herb.

"Encante visium," Camilla whispered and swallowed the herb. Thankfully, the spell worked and Camilla could faintly see outlines of cave walls and curvatures and crevices in the rocks all around her. She sighed in relief—she'd never tried that spell before. Today was a day of firsts.

Although sight didn't necessarily make it any better. Now she could just see the creepiness all around her. But at least she wouldn't bump into walls.

Isabelle was so focused on her task that she didn't hear or didn't care about Camilla's spell happening behind her. She continued walking steadfastly down the long, lightless tunnel. Isabelle's back was straight, her head held high. Camilla was hunched over, almost hiding behind her co-conspirator. The anticipation of what they would find when they got to Bianca was almost overwhelming to Camilla. She just told herself to trust in her plan. It was all she could do.

After what felt like the longest walk in history, they came to a fork in the path.

"Which way?" Isabelle asked, her voice barely above a whisper.

Camilla closed her eyes and tried to tune into the spell she had performed early this morning to find Bianca's cave in the first place. She willed the magic to guide them either right or left. She sensed the direction and then opened her eyes. But before she could tell Isabelle what she'd sensed, a voice cut through the darkness and echoed off the cave walls.

"Looking for me?"

Camilla swallowed hard. Her senses had been right. Down the tunnel to the right, Bianca was waiting for them.

†††

"These must be their footprints." Elias pointed to the mud beneath their feet. He looked other-worldly, standing there in the sunlight with his black hood and cape.

Shane nodded. He could normally sense

Camilla as easy as breathing, but today it was all cloudy and distorted as if he were trying to see her in a funhouse mirror. He knew she was deliberately making it harder for him to track her, and it frustrated him. The desire to protect her and Isabelle was making him almost feral. "Let's follow them. They were here not long ago, or the location spell wouldn't have dropped us here."

"Does anyone else think we look like the start of a joke? Two monks and a surfer walk into a bar..." Luke chuckled at his own joke while Shane just shook his head. Elias remained stoic. He probably didn't understand the humor.

"This way." And Shane pointed up a hill nearby.

"Is this a search and rescue? Or will we confront Bianca?" Elias asked as calmly as if he were asking about the weather. Soldier through and through.

Shane continued walking at superhuman speed. He didn't turn around but he answered over his shoulder where Elias and Luke were trailing. "The plan is search and rescue, but if we face Bianca, we ask her what we need to know." After a pause he added, "And I'll do the talking, Luke."

Luke raised his hands in response as if to say, "Who, me?"

Elias ignored him and stated to Shane's shoulder, "I hope they haven't entered Bianca's lair, then. That will make this much harder."

"Better pick up speed." Shane went from a superhuman walk to vampire-speed running, leaving a blur behind him. Elias and Luke did the same. They didn't stop when they reached the bottom of the hill that Camilla and Isabelle had climbed minutes ago. They continued at top speed as they ascended the hill, caring much less than the girls had about stepping on leaves and shrubbery. Shane knew he had to get there before something happened.

When they reached the top of the hill, they were greeted with the same dark cave.

"They didn't go in there, did they?" Luke asked.

Shane said nothing but did a quick glance around. There were a few trees, but not many. There were no homes or structures. There was nowhere else they could be. He steeled himself against the sense of foreboding and stepped into the void.

"This should be loads of fun," Luke said, rolling his eyes as he and Elias followed Shane into the dark cavern.

✝✝✝

"Well don't be rude. Come on in," Bianca called from the tunnel. The sound of water dripping still echoed throughout the chamber. Camilla felt the temperature drop a few degrees and she suddenly felt the air that never saw sunlight. Isabelle looked at Camilla, who nodded in return. This was why they were here. And Isabelle still didn't know it, but Camilla knew they were running out of head start.

Isabelle walked cautiously down the dark tunnel. She didn't know what trap could await her. She had no idea what she was about to face. None of them did. The tunnel was maybe ten feet, but it felt like the longest march ever. Camilla took deep breaths to keep her hammering heart from giving her away. When Isabelle rounded the corner from the tunnel and entered the chamber where Bianca lay in waiting, Camilla hung back, hiding behind the cave wall.

Isabelle stepped boldly into the cavern. There were soft glows of light reflecting off cutouts in the rock. It wasn't fire, but some sort of stone or element that glowed. It dimly lit a large chamber with high ceilings. The walls were rugged. Isabelle assumed Bianca had moved into an existing cavern, rather than something she formed or created.

"I so rarely get visitors. To what do I owe this absolute pleasure?" Bianca was sitting on a stone bench that very much resembled a throne. She was scantily clad in an evening gown that had long since had its heyday. It was tattered and hanging in places it shouldn't. Bianca didn't seem to care. A young man was kissing her neck and she shoved him off her and stood.

Isabelle watched him fall to the floor. He was chained around the neck and pale, gaunt. He must have been her feeder. There were a dozen other bodies chained around the room, Isabelle suddenly noticed, mostly women. All were staring silently and moving slowly, as if they were drugged or, more likely, so low on blood they were barely alive.

"I'm here about the Dark Prophecy." Isabelle stood as tall as she could and spoke confidently.

Bianca slithered slowly over to Isabelle, a wicked grin on her lips. As she neared, Isabelle was surprised to see she looked young. In her imagination, Bianca had been an old woman. The woman before her was a beauty, albeit one in desperate need of indoor plumbing. Her brown hair was a tangled mess, but her skin was smooth like porcelain. She had high cheekbones and full lips. There was a classic Audrey-Hepburn-style beauty to her. When she finally made her way to Isabelle, she slid a long finger with claws fully extended down Isabelle's face, and then she leaned in and kissed Isabelle's lips.

Isabelle had been preparing herself for days for a battle, but nowhere in her thoughts had she expected someone with the reputation of Bianca to kiss her. She stumbled back in surprise.

"You're cute. I think you can stay." Bianca grabbed Isabelle's wrist and pulled her toward the stone throne. Her grip was forceful and strong. Isabelle had never known such strength. And she was still reeling from the surprise kiss. "You know I normally kill outsiders."

"Yes, but this is important," Isabelle tried to explain as Bianca pulled her onto her lap.

"Shhhh." Bianca stuck her dirty claw up to Isabelle's lips.

"What exactly are you doing?" Isabelle wiggled, but Bianca held her on her lap like a vise.

"It's been decades since I got a new pet. I'm so glad you came to me," Bianca purred and nuzzled into Isabelle's neck. Sensing she was losing control of the situation fast, Isabelle again used her considerable strength to get free. She had come for a fight, but this had caught her completely off guard. She hadn't worked hard to become an elite vampire warrior only to die as a love toy for some sadistic old bitch.

"I came here to find out how to stop the Dark Prophecy." Isabelle pulled her arms, trying to free them. No luck.

"Are you here alone?" Bianca sniffed along Isabelle's neck and then looked into her eyes. Bianca's eyes were as dark as the cave she lived in. She was nothing anymore but a black widow spider, eating whatever was trapped in her web.

But as Isabelle stared into Bianca's eyes, she felt her arms get heavy. She felt almost tired, very calm. Why had she been fighting? This was peaceful. Was she here alone? No, that's right. Camilla. Isabelle's mind was fuzzy and filling with heaviness. Should she be protecting Camilla? No. She needed to be honest with the woman who was giving her love and peace.

"No," she answered, and her voice sounded loopy and far away to her own ears. What was happening? This didn't seem right.

"I knew it. You brought a witch. I can smell her." Bianca hissed the words, long and drawn out. She sniffed the air and then laughed. But her laughter was maniacal, anything but jovial. "How kind of you to bring me a snack. I haven't had witch's blood in a century." She licked her lips and ran her tongue along her long, extended fangs, the thought of witch's blood making her very hungry.

She gently placed Isabelle on the cold ground and began slinking toward Camilla's hiding spot. Isabelle couldn't explain why, but she didn't want Bianca to leave her. Wordlessly she reached out to the vampire who had made her feel so secure. Hadn't she been here for a fight? Why did she want to hug Bianca so badly?

"Let her go." Shane's voice echoed throughout the chamber.

Through her fear, Camilla smiled to herself. It was clear that Bianca had been caught off guard by Shane, distracted by Isabelle and Camilla.

Maybe they had a small chance after all.

Bianca turned toward the new voice. Clearly at the fork in the path, Shane and his team had gone the other way and found another entrance. But she didn't hesitate for long. "A whole group of visitors. I'm so flattered."

Without turning away from Shane, she reached around the cave opening and grabbed Camilla by the throat. "Thank you for the offering. I love the little feisty one. She'll make a lovely addition to my collection." Isabelle giggled at Bianca's words. *Feisty one.* What was *wrong* with her? "And this one." Bianca pulled Camilla's hair until her neck was fully exposed, caressing it with her other claw. Shane tried to remain stoic, but his nostrils flared in frustration. And Bianca was watching him like a hawk. "How'd you know I love the taste of witches?"

"Elias! Now!" Shane shouted the order. Elias was supposed to attack her and pull her focus so Shane could overpower her with fire or water. Only Elias didn't move. Not one inch. Shane looked over his shoulder and saw the same loopy look on his face that Isabelle was wearing. A glance over his other shoulder told him that Luke had the same expression.

As Shane realized they were tranced by Bianca, Bianca watched his realization dawn and laughed to herself. What a fun day this turned out to be. "I see you are unaffected by my powers. I take it that means you are someone special. And the witch is special to you." She pulled Camilla's hair again for good measure and Camilla winced at the pain. She tried to keep her breathing calm in Bianca's clutches, but she had no control over it. She was petrified and her heart was echoing that fear throughout the cave. It was like a siren's song to this ancient vampire holding her tight. Bianca moved her fangs to a hair's breadth above Camilla's neck and said, "This should raise the stakes of the game a bit."

"This isn't a game, Bianca. Let her go," Shane instructed, his voice full of confidence. He was certain he could kill Bianca, but that wasn't why he was here. Ultimately, he needed information. And Camilla caught in the middle, endangering her life, was exactly what he didn't want to have happen. This was all wrong.

And Bianca didn't seem to care anyway. She'd kill Camilla just to provoke him. Old, bored and pure evil.

"I know. The feisty one told me. You're here about the prophecy. Always the useless prophecy." Bianca threw Camilla to the floor, keeping her hair in her clutches as she dragged Camilla back to her throne of stone. It took every ounce of restraint Shane had not to overreact and play into Bianca's hands. Camilla struggled uselessly to get free, but she controlled herself well considering the circumstances. She was a powerful and clever witch, but she still needed her hands and her potions in order to cast a spell.

When Bianca reached her throne, Shane watched as a giggly Isabelle ran to her side, watching the old vampire as if she were a rock star. Her every move amazed Isabelle. And Shane had never seen Isabelle like this. It was horrific.

"You and I are both very powerful, Bianca.

Let's just talk. These girls snuck up here on their own. They were just trying to impress me," Shane stated.

Bianca laughed hysterically at this, forcing Camilla's head far forward as she continued pulling her hair even as she laughed. When she finally stopped laughing, her face became hard—her cheekbones jutting so strongly out of her face they almost appeared like weapons, her eyes fierce as lightning. "I've thanked you for my gifts. Now be gone. I have no interest in you."

Shane stepped toward Bianca. His patience was wearing thin, and a small display of powers might be needed in order to get her to start talking. "I'm not leaving without Isabelle and Camilla." He formed a small fireball in his right hand and then tossed it back and forth between his hands. "And I need information."

"Cute parlor trick," Bianca said and yanked on Camilla's hair, pulling the young witch onto her lap. "Now leave, or I drain her life force right here in front of you before pulling off the other's one head so I can drink her blood from her neck." To show she wasn't kidding, Bianca extended her fangs and again leaned in toward Camilla's neck. Camilla squeezed her eyes shut, complete terror overtaking her.

Shane looked at Camilla only for a second. He had to get her out of here. The witches' regeneration potion might keep her from dying but he had no idea what the effect would be on Camilla, or what Bianca would do when Camilla kept getting up after being drained of blood. At the end of the day, powerful witch or not, she was still mortal.

And Shane still loved her.

"Release the witch," Shane shouted to the old vampire. Wrong answer.

In an instant, Bianca sunk her teeth into Camilla and the witch's body went limp. Shane reacted before thinking, sending a powerful wave of air toward Bianca and knocking her backward. The old vampire lost her grip on Camilla and flew back, hitting the stone wall and crumpling onto the cave floor. Camilla landed in a heap where she'd been dropped, although at the last minute Shane sent a gust of air to cushion the blow. It was all he could do at that moment. He had to stay focused on Bianca. In his anger, Shane sent a fireball at Bianca's feet, setting her legs ablaze.

"Bianca!" Isabelle cried, her shoulder racked with sobs.

Shane walked slowly over to Bianca. He didn't really want this to go too much further, but this vampire was so unpredictable. Again he was surprised at her reaction.

Bianca laughed, loud and strong, as she patted the flames with her bare hands, extinguishing the fire that ravaged her legs. Her charred stumps sat there as she looked up to Shane with a wicked gleam in her eyes. "Well, well. The Chosen One wants to fight, huh? This day is turning out to be far more exciting than I'd expected."

4

It was midday and Emily knew her sister would be sleeping like the dead. Or the undead. Or whatever she was. But there was no way she could do this without at least telling her sister. Kara would never forgive her for that.

The curtains were drawn although some light was creeping through, giving the room more of a soft glow than complete darkness or light. Emily crept in, closing the door to the third-floor bedroom behind her. She knew it was a little bit creepy, but she sat on the bed and watched her little sister sleep. Like this, it was easy to see the little girl she'd once been and not the vampire she'd become.

Kara had never been a saint. She was devious

from the get-go, lying to their parents at age three when there wasn't even a reason to lie. Maybe she was always destined to be something aggressive, but Emily remembered the simple things like playing dress-up or playing with dolls. And the first time she'd put make-up on her baby sister, Kara had looked like a clown, but she walked around feeling like a supermodel, bright blue eyeshadow drowning her lids and taking over her eyebrows, red lipstick shooting way past her lips. Emily smiled at the memory.

With one last glance at her angelic sleeping face, Emily shook her sister. She wasn't entirely sure that would work to wake a vampire. She'd never done that before. Hell, she'd never even imagined she'd know a vampire, let alone live amongst them, her sister one of them. It was all back to Theresa. She'd stolen their innocence when she murdered their mother and brought witchcraft into their peaceful family home in the harbor.

She shook her sister again, this time a bit harder, and then jumped back as it had its intended affect. Kara woke up, fangs extended ready to attack whatever had awakened her.

Realizing what was happening, Kara let her fangs retract. "Emily! I might've killed you."

"Give me a little credit. I might be a new witch but I'm learning new things every day. I'm not scared of you." Emily smiled at her sister.

Kara was still a little grumpy from being awakened by surprise. She ran a hand across her face. "What do you want, Em?"

"I'm going to find dad. And I didn't want to leave without telling you. I'll be back in a few days," Emily told her sister.

Kara groaned. "Emily, that life is over. Hasn't that poor man been through enough? Now he has to find out that his daughter is a witch? Oh, and the one you thought ran away is actually a vampire? Let him grieve and move on. He's better off not knowing what happened to us."

Emily shook her head. "I can't let him suffer another loss when we're both perfectly fine."

"Perfectly fine?"

"Theresa lived as a witch under his nose. He never suspected a thing." Emily shifted so her full body was facing Kara on the bed. "And we can tell him you have some kind of disease that keeps you out of the sun."

"First of all, Theresa should never be used as an example of anything." Kara lay back down on her pillow. "And he'll never believe us. He'll know it's all a lie."

"So maybe we tell him the truth?" Emily asked with a shrug. "It will take time to process, but then he won't constantly be wondering and questioning."

"He'll be horrified and leave us again," Kara answered.

"But that will be his choice. At least he'll know," Emily responded.

Kara tossed her covers back and climbed out of bed. "For the record, I think this is one of the stupidest ideas you've ever had." Kara pulled on pants underneath her nightgown.

"But?" Emily asked.

Kara looked back over her shoulder at her sister. "But if you're going no matter what, I'm going with you."

Kara finished getting dressed and the two girls headed down the stairs to Emily's room. If Kara was coming, they would need another cloak. Henna was sitting on her bed in the room they shared, and she looked up when the two girls walked in. Her legs were crossed at her ankles and her back was straight as a line.

"Can I borrow a cloak from you for Kara?" Emily asked.

Henna raised one eyebrow questioningly. "What happened to yours?'

"I had to give them to Elias and Luke so they could go with Shane to rescue Isabelle and Camilla," Emily stated flatly, as if heading off on a major excursion to face a deadly ancient vampire was an everyday activity. Of course, for all she knew it was.

"What happened to Isabelle?" Kara asked with

shock in her voice. Isabelle was her idol and mentor. Yes, her sister was her sister, but in many ways Isabelle had become like a sister too. Instant worry for Isabelle put tension into every muscle of Kara's undead body. She coiled like snake ready to strike.

"Well, it was kind of Isabelle's fault, really." Emily frowned as she explained to the two girls. "Isabelle snuck off with Camilla to go face Bianca, some old vampire. I don't know much of the details except Shane was really worried."

Kara relaxed a little at that. "Oh. Shane's always worried, so that doesn't mean anything necessarily. He has some skills and all, but he needs to relax a bit." She snickered a bit at her own joke. Her real dad might be wandering the streets of Los Angeles half-mad, but Shane was so overprotective she'd never had to miss having a father figure.

"Do you realize how much you owe to my brother?" Julianna suddenly appeared in the doorway. For a human, she sure was able to sneak in quietly and undetected. She was clutching something to her chest and looking at Kara, Emily and Henna with large, worried eyes. In fact, her expression reminded them very much of Shane. "If he relaxes for even a minute, someone is always trying to kidnap, steal or kill one of us. Imagine being just a kid one day and then have every vampire's well-being as your responsibility the next."

At least Kara had the decency to look embarrassed by her previous words. The truth was, she loved Shane. And she didn't want to be him for one second, so she knew Julianna was right.

Instead of an apology or acknowledging any of Julianna's words, Emily asked, "Do you think Camilla and Isabelle will be okay?"

Julianna sighed. Her face was so soft now, she really did look like a human. "If anyone can save them, Shane can. But Bianca is infamous. She's the kind of vampire even vampires are scared of."

Kara snorted. "She can't be any kind of threat to Isabelle."

Julianna contorted her mouth in a way that

showed she felt Kara was very naïve. "Isabelle is one of the fiercest I've ever met. But Bianca has killed vampires tougher than her for centuries. Only Shane can match Bianca."

A heavy silence filled the air for a moment, everyone pondering the seriousness of Julianna's words.

"Then why on earth would they go on their own?" Henna asked. Her voice was so regal. She wasn't necessarily cunning like Theresa and Camilla, but Julianna could easily imagine this witch running her own coven one day. She held her head so high, neck so long, just like a Queen.

"They wanted to protect Shane." Julianna shook her head. "But they don't realize how much they've jeopardized instead."

"No." Henna stood up, calmly but boldly. "Camilla is way too smart. She has a master plan, believe me."

"I hope so." Julianna smiled softly, but it was sad, as if she was saying the words but didn't really believe they had a glimmer of hope.

"No, you're right, Henna. Camilla has a plan. She doesn't do anything impulsively," Emily added a little too insistently.

"Do we go after them?" Kara asked, her fangs beginning to extend, her body prepped for a fight again.

"No, you'll only make things worse," Julianna said.

"I agree," Henna added. "Whatever you were planning to do today with my cloak, just stick to that plan."

Emily smiled. That was something they could do that would be productive. No sense in worrying about some vamps on a mission. "We're going to find our dad."

Julianna sucked in a breath that expressed her dissent before she could quickly recover and pretend she didn't care. Damn human emotions! She clutched the book she was holding tighter to her chest. Emily looked at Julianna but said nothing.

"I think it's stupid too," Kara announced, looking at Julianna.

Julianna didn't respond right away. She looked down at the book she'd been clutching and then sighed again before she spoke, attempting to put words to the thoughts and emotions swirling around in her brain. "I wouldn't use the word 'stupid'. More like reckless." She held the book out to the ladies she was with. "This is my diary. My old diary from my old human life. Shane had it."

"Wow," Emily said. It was all any of them could think to say.

"I've been reading it and enjoying the memories, but it's like reading about someone else's life. It *is* someone else's life." Julianna looked up at Emily and Kara. "I'm human again, but still, this isn't me anymore. That Julianna died. My parents buried her. She's gone. Do you see what I mean?"

"I don't know how she did it, but Theresa murdered my mom so she could marry my dad," Emily stated with her arms folded. Kara hissed. "And then, because of Theresa, Kara was turned to a vampire. Theresa took everything from that man, and he doesn't even know a fraction of the truth. Hell, he doesn't even know his wife is dead."

"She poisoned her," Henna said, her lips tight. "Witches have many ways of disposing of people, but if they want it to look natural, they use witch hazel mixed with nightshade. It stops the heart and makes it look like a heart attack."

Kara narrowed her eyes and let her claws extend. "And you know this how?"

If Henna was intimidated by the vampire in her presence, she didn't let it show. "I was in her coven. I knew Theresa well. She didn't exactly share her plans of murder with us, but I knew it all along." She shrugged a small shrug. "It's one of the oldest tricks in the book."

Kara's shoulders heaved up and down heavily and her fangs elongated. "There are too many humans in here and I need to bite something now."

Julianna held out her wrist. "Bite me. You can't

kill me thanks to the witches." Kara reached for Julianna's arm, but Emily batted her out of the way.

"Are you crazy? Shane would kill you if you bit his sister," Emily scolded Kara.

Henna rolled her eyes. "Bite me, then. I have the same protection."

Before Emily could object again, Kara sank her fangs deep into Henna's flesh. Emily tried to hide the look of horror on her face, but it was hard to see her sister acting so much like...well, like a vampire.

Finally, Emily stepped in. "Okay, that's enough."

Kara let some of Henna's blood drip down her chin before she licked it up with her tongue. Henna rubbed her wrist, but the wounds healed quickly without need of a bandage.

"I wish Camilla hadn't killed her so completely. I want to resurrect her so I can kill her again. This time kill her myself!" Kara looked around the room and then grabbed something to hurl at the wall.

"Calm down, Kara." Emily rubbed her sister's

shoulders, encouraging her to tone down the aggression.

Julianna leaned against the doorframe. "See what I mean? Reckless."

"How you decide to handle your parents is your decision," Emily said to Julianna, still rubbing Kara's shoulders. "But it's our decision how to handle our dad."

Kara was calming, but she still breathed heavily and her fangs were still extended. "Theresa might be dead, but I can still tell my dad all about her and what she really was. Then I can kill her reputation."

"Suit yourself. It *is* your decision," Julianna said. "But prepare yourself for the repercussions." And she turned and left the room.

"Give me the cloak, I'm ready," Kara said to Henna.

"I'll get you the cloak, but I'm coming too," Henna said, her arms folded across her chest.

Emily gently placed a hand on her friend's arm. She was coming to really love and respect this dark-haired witch. "I appreciate your support, but this is family business."

"And I'm not entirely sure what our misfit coven is doing in a vampire compound or how long it could possibly last, but I do know one thing. We *are* a family. A half witch, half vampire, bizarre, eccentric, mixed up and coo-coo family," Henna's tone was deadly serious. "So I'm coming too."

Emily smiled. It did feel like things might've changed, as Julianna mentioned, and old lives were gone for good. But this new life came with a new family, and that was still very much real.

The three ladies left: two witches and a vampire hidden under a cloak, heading for the streets of downtown Los Angeles.

5

"I don't want to fight. I want to talk." Shane let Bianca stand up, but he remained close and at the ready. He didn't trust her.

Bianca rested a hand on Shane's chest. The gesture would've been flirtatious, only Bianca was anything but coy. It came across more like she wanted to lull Shane into a false sense of security, only to try something at the last minute. Without breaking eye contact, Shane removed her hand.

"I never thought I'd live to see the day," Bianca hissed. She began to walk back toward her throne, where Isabelle and Camilla still remained. "And really, that's why I live in a cave. I didn't want to see the day." She looked back over her shoulder at Shane.

"Then tell us what we need to know and we'll go," Shane said, following the old vampire. He didn't want her near the girls without him close enough to stop whatever she might try. "How do we stop the second part of the prophecy?"

But instead, she laughed. Tossed her Audrey-Hepburn-looking hair back and laughed heartily.

"No one can stop it. Not even you." She waved a finger at Luke and he stumbled like a zombie over to her. She pulled him into her lap. "Can I at least keep this one?"

Shane stepped in front of Bianca, seated on her throne of stone. He pushed Isabelle and Camilla behind him, although Isabelle stepped back around. If Bianca got out of her sight, she got very anxious. Whatever spell Bianca was spinning was really starting to annoy Shane. "If you can't tell us how to stop it, then we have no use for you. We'll leave you to your cave."

She ran her fingers through Luke's hair, sniffing his neck. Shane tensed as her fangs neared his best friend's body. "Apparently you don't know how prophecies are made." She stopped threatening Luke long enough to look back at Shane. "A seer has seen the prophecy. It's not a prediction. It's a *history* that hasn't yet come to pass."

"If it hasn't happened yet, it can still be stopped," Shane stated.

Bianca waved a finger at Shane. "Ah, ah. Look what happened to Dimas when he tried to change the prophecy. It never ends well for those who fight what will come to pass."

"So we just let the vampires die out?" Shane asked, staring at this creature before him caressing Luke. She didn't seem like someone who would complacently let her twisted way of living disappear.

In a flash, she shoved Luke to the ground and appeared inches from Shane's face. "What are you so afraid of?"

Not backing down, Shane inched even closer, shoving his nose to hers to show he wasn't afraid. He had to keep his eyes away from Luke, Elias, and Isabelle or he could lose control. "The vampires are my responsibility. I'm not letting their existence end."

This made Bianca laugh all the harder. "I admire your delusional nobility." She pulled Isabelle close to her and caressed her right in front of Shane. She knew his need to protect his friends, and she was enjoying pushing the buttons. "But they're not your responsibility. Your role has been played. And those events have led to the current events. And these lead to what will come to pass. You can't stop it because you *started* it."

He heard Camilla suck in a breath behind him. It only served to make him more confused. And the confusion was fueling his anger. "I don't believe you. We're leaving."

Bianca sat back down on her throne, crossing her legs and attempting to appear as a seductress. Without her trancing ability, though, it was wasted on Shane. He found her disgusting. "I can tell you everything you need to know, but I expect to be paid for my troubles."

"If I can't stop it, there's nothing more to talk

about."

"I said I could tell you what you *need* to know. Not what you *want* to know." Bianca leaned back and smiled wickedly. She let her fangs extend slowly. "And I want the pretty witch as my payment."

Shane's blood boiled and he fought the urge to kill this ancient vampire right then and there. But they could just leave. This whole adventure had been completely useless. "Not happening."

Shane grabbed Luke and pulled him to his feet. He was likely going to have to carry him and Isabelle. They were both so entranced with Bianca they would never walk out on their own accord. Elias still stood dumbly in the front of the cave. Would he come willingly, or would Shane have to carry him too?

"It's okay, Shane. I'll stay."

Shane looked over his shoulder as Camilla, toying with her hair, walked slowly toward Bianca. He started to object, but then saw the look in her eyes. She had a plan, and he knew better than to underestimate her. He fumed as his desire to protect her warred with his complete faith in her.

No matter how cunning she was, this was still Bianca. And he didn't trust Bianca.

"Finally, someone sees reason." Bianca yanked on Camilla's arm, forcing her onto her lap. She extended a claw and caressed Camilla's cheek with it. "She's pretty. I see why you wanted to keep her for yourself, Chosen One."

The poisonous flower. Camilla looked so vulnerable and beautiful on Bianca's lap, he fought the urge to grab her, run away with her and live on the farm Julianna mentioned. Leaving all this behind.

Shane stood up straight, leaving Luke wobbling at his side. Isabelle had inched closer to Bianca, still acting like a schoolgirl and making Shane do a double-take. It was disconcerting to see Isabelle acting this way, so unlike herself.

"All right. You have the witch." Shane glanced at Camilla but then looked quickly back at Bianca, worried that his feelings might give him away. "What is it you feel I need to know?"

Through smiling fangs, Bianca sunk her teeth deep into Camilla's neck. Shane started forward, but Camilla held up her hand to tell him to stop. She winced at the pain, but knew she was protected by the rejuvenation spell. Shane looked at Bianca and fought the urge to rip her head from her body. He'd never wanted to hit a woman so badly, even if the woman was an evil vampire as old as the dust in the cave.

Another minute and Camilla would be lifeless. Shane could take it no longer and pulled Camilla away from Bianca. "Enough with the games, Bianca. We're leaving."

Bianca licked the dripping blood from her chin and shrugged. "I don't get many visitors. Can't a girl have some fun?"

Shane lifted Isabelle over his shoulder and pulled Luke. He could walk, just did so like a drunk man. Shane hoped once they were out of the cave, the trance would end. He had no idea what to expect, as he'd never seen a vampire entrance other vampires before. With Camilla holding his other hand, he stormed toward Elias, hoping he could also walk on his own.

But he didn't make it all the way to Elias. A force from behind knocked Shane to the cave floor, sending Isabelle flying off his shoulder and pushing Camilla and Luke also to their knees.

Bianca. She was way more powerful than he'd given her credit for.

Bianca laughed. "Thought you were the only one that could control the air, did you?"

6

Downtown Los Angeles in the middle of the afternoon was alive with energy. Cars honked as other cars darted in front of them. There were people everywhere. People in cars. People on bikes. People walking the streets. In restaurants, heading into office buildings, working out in gyms.

"How are we going to find him? I haven't smelled him yet as a vampire," Kara explained, taking in a big breath from under her witch's cloak. They stood at the edge of the parking garage, hidden in the shadows. Luckily enough, people were eccentric around these parts. Some might stare at Kara's garb, but most would likely assume she was some weirdo and go about their selfish ways.

"We're witches, remember?   Locator spell." Emily smiled at her sister and held up one of their dad's ties. "He came down here looking for you, but he has pretty much lost his mind."

"Looking for me? Here?" Kara was shocked.

Henna nodded. "Based on Theresa's cover story for your disappearance. She told him you'd run away with a boy."

"What bullshit. I can't believe he fell for it," Kara said.

"He questioned it a bit, but I corroborated it and then he believed." Emily dropped her gaze, her embarrassment plastered on her face.

"Theresa was controlling you too. Don't worry about it," Kara told her sister. "Let bygones be bygones."

"Well, and what were they going to say? Kara is a vampire now, get over it?" Henna folded her graceful arms across her chest. Kara just shrugged in response.

Emily flicked a lighter from her pocket, since

she didn't have Shane to create a flame with his powers, and started the locator spell. "When we find him, we tell him everything. I promise."

The spell led them down Sixth Street to San Pedro. They turned into another parking structure where homeless people were milling about. The thought of their father just giving up on life and living on the streets made no sense. But they saw him there. His beard was grown out, his clothes tattered. There was a darkness in his eyes, but they were still his.

"Dad!" Emily shouted. A few random homeless men staggered their way over to Emily, one even volunteering to be her father. So she changed her tactic. "Richard!"

Richard saw them but made no move in their direction. Instead, he sat on the ground and leaned against a cement wall.

"It's like a hangover," Henna explained. "He was essentially drugged by Theresa for so many years, and then he quit cold turkey. He might not be able to come even if he wanted to."

Before Emily could decide what to do about her spell-withdrawing father, a security guard from the parking structure came by and told all the homeless they had to leave. Her heart squeezed a bit for all these people that had nowhere to go, but she had to remain focused on her father. She couldn't let him wander off, assuming he even could, with the homeless gang he was running with.

"This one is mine," Emily explained to the security guard, gesturing to her father sitting on the ground.

"Just get him out of here," the guard responded.

Emily nodded and then ran to her father, kneeling at his feet. Kara and Henna came up behind her, standing over Emily and Richard. Kara's robe cast a shadow on her face, but Richard looked up, squinting into the hood, and seemed to recognize the figure that hid under there.

"Kara? Is that you? Lower your hood." Richard's words slurred together like a drunk man. His head wobbled as he strained to continue looking at the face under the hood.

"She can't, Dad," Emily explained. "Can you stand? You have to come with me, and we'll explain everything."

"No." Richard swatted at the air in front of him, missing whatever he wanted to hit and falling over with the momentum. "I'm not ready to go back to Theresa. Something's not right with her."

Emily looked up at Kara and Henna. Henna shrugged but Kara announced with little emotion or fanfare, "Theresa's dead. Now let's get out of here before I roast in the sun or eat somebody."

"Dead?" His faced expressed confusion more than anything. He must've assumed Kara was kidding about eating someone.

"I'll help you stand. We can't port out of here with the security guard watching us," Emily instructed. She started to lift one side, getting nowhere, when Kara walked over and lifted him, tossing him over her shoulder like he weighed nothing.

"Super strength. That's handy." Emily smiled

at her sister. Deciding it was best to not walk along the streets in broad daylight with a man over the shoulder of someone in a black hooded robe, they gathered behind a dumpster in an alley. From there, Emily and Henna could transport them back to the compound.

Once they were safely inside Kara's room, Kara removed her robe and looked on her father with vampire eyes for the first time. He looked and smelled horrible. *Good*, she thought. It would save her from wanting to drink his blood.

Without even acknowledging he was back with Kara, he asked, "How did Theresa die?"

"Long story," Kara responded.

"First, we need to get your mind out of that haze," Emily said, standing up straight.

"I know a potion we could use," Henna announced, and Emily nodded in her direction. Kara didn't want to trust Henna, but she trusted Emily, so no one argued, and Henna left to get the potion to clear his head. "You can stay with us until you're ready to go home."

"Home?" Richard asked, his face wrinkling up as he tried to remember where he lived.

Emily sat next to her father and placed a gentle hand on his knee. "Yes. You have a beautiful home in Ventura. Don't you remember?"

"I remember..." His voice trailed off as he tried to clear his own mind of the cobwebs that had been formed by magic. "I remember the two of you...and then we lost your mother and I was so lonely. So lonely." He looked up at Kara. "And then we lost you too. Why did you run off?"

Kara looked at Emily as if to ask if it was okay to start in with the full story. Emily shook her head and said, "We'll explain everything when Henna gets back with your potion."

"Potion?"

"It's a magical drink that will clear your head," Emily explained. Kara just kept pacing, nervous energy spilling off her.

Moments later, Henna walked in with a red plastic cup that appeared to be smoking. Julianna followed fast on her heels. Emily looked at her but said nothing. As Shane's sister, she held a lot of weight and Emily wasn't going to be the one to tell her to get out.

Henna handed the cup to Emily and Emily knelt before her father. "Drink this. It will clear your mind."

Richard stared at it as he took the cup from his daughter. He sniffed it and then looked at Emily once more before taking a tiny sip. His head still wobbled and his words still slurred. "Potion?"

"Trust me," Emily said and pushed the cup to his lips once more. "This potion will counteract the potions Theresa was slipping you for years. She was a witch, Dad."

Richard spit out the small bit of liquid he had in his mouth. "What?"

Emily encouraged him to drink more, nodding at him.

"We said we'd tell you everything, Dad," Kara began, still pacing, "but you have to know that some things we're going to tell you are going to seem crazy. Theresa being a witch is probably the least of them, to be honest."

Whether he believed them or was just simply thirsty from living on the streets, Richard did finally take a decent swig of the potion Henna had prepared.

After a moment, Emily started in. "I'm a witch too. So is Henna." She gestured at her graceful, dark-skinned friend.

"And I suppose that means you ran off because you are a witch too?" Richard asked Kara.

Kara made a gagging sound. "Gross. I'm a vampire."

Richard started to laugh, but then he looked at the faces all around him. No one seemed to be joking.

"Theresa picked a fight with vampires, and they used me and Kara to get back at her. They turned Kara and then I joined the witches for revenge. But ultimately, everyone on both sides realized that the biggest problem was Theresa. She was murdered by a fellow witch," Emily explained.

"Murdered?" Richard looked at Emily, who nodded in response, her face as serious as he'd ever seen. He wasn't sure his mind was clear enough to process everything, so he took another drink of the potion. It did seem to be sobering him, even though he never remembered drinking any alcohol. "So I've now lost two wives?"

"Nothing with Theresa was real, Dad," Kara said.

Henna jumped in. "She slipped you love potion every day in your orange juice. You were just a pawn. A victim like the rest of us."

Emily added, "You can stay here with us, or you can try to go back to your old life, but please know that Kara, at least, can't ever go back. And, honestly, I'm not sure I want to."

Julianna spoke for the first time. "When you become a vampire, you have to die first. Kara is undead. There is no life for her to go back to."

Richard looked at the young, pretty blonde. "Are you a witch too?"

"No, I'm just a regular human," Julianna responded. Richard seemed to relax his shoulders at the thought of another normal person in the room with him. "I *was* a vampire, but I was killed and resurrected by the witches as a human."

Richard looked at Emily. At least she was a familiar face that appeared to be human. "How is any of this possible?"

But it was Kara who answered. "I warned you this was crazy."

Richard shook his head, trying to clear it from all the words he was hearing that didn't make sense. Jumbled with a fog from years of being bewitched, his mind just wouldn't let everything combine into a cohesive story. Theresa murdered...witches and vampires...they can't go home. "You keep saying I can stay here. Where is here?"

Julianna rolled her eyes. "This should be fun."

Emily looked back at Shane's sister. "I swore I would be honest and tell him everything." She looked back at her father with kind eyes. He loved his daughter completely and trusted her wholeheartedly, but the way she was looking at him sent a shiver down his spine. "This is a vampire compound, once the home of the Strashni vampires. When Shane united all the vampires, the individual vampire tribes went away, and he welcomed all vampires and witches to live here."

"You said a lot of words in that, Emily, but most of them make no sense," Richard said. Sure, there was a lot of fog still fumigating his brain, but he felt certain that even without the haze of magic he wouldn't understand completely.

"There's no reason to give him the full rundown on the prophecy." Kara folded her arms.

"So, I'm in a house with a bunch of vampires and witches?" Richard asked, not even able to begin to wonder about a prophecy.

"And one human," Julianna held up a hand. "Well, now, two."

Richard looked at Kara. She'd always been a handful, pushing her limits and diving headfirst into any situation, but this was beyond even his wildest imaginations of where she'd end up. "You eat people?"

"No," Kara responded quickly. "I *drink* people."

"Okay, okay," Emily said, cutting that conversation short. No reason to put images in her father's head of his youngest daughter drinking blood. But it seemed too late. He placed his head in his hands and looked like he might start crying. "Let's give you a moment to rest and recover. You've had quite the afternoon."

Richard's body went stiff at Emily's words. "I don't want to be left alone in a house full of witches and vampires."

"No one's going to hurt you, dad," Emily stated.

"I'll protect you," Kara added. "And don't worry, you smell too nasty for any of us to want to eat you."

A small knock on the door put everyone in the room on edge. The vampires should be sleeping, and most witches wouldn't brave coming to Kara's room on the third floor. After looks of confusion were exchanged—no one seemed to be expecting anyone— Henna walked over and answered it.

Collette, the witch who had first stood up to Theresa, seemed a bit nervous standing there in the doorway.

"Hi, Collette," Henna greeted her coven sister. She hadn't expected her, but she was happy to see her.

Collette's eyes swung cautiously over to Julianna. "I have something for the chosen one's sister."

In super vampire speed, Kara appeared at the doorway, prepared to protect Shane's sister from any potential threat. "What is it?"

Julianna pushed through Kara and Henna, who stood in the doorway, blocking Collette from the others. "Relax. I'm loosely a part of the coven too. I trust Collette."

"It's a message for you, Julianna." Collette held out a small piece of paper, one that had been folded many times over.

Julianna unfolded the paper and read it carefully. When she finished, she looked up at Collette, then at Kara and Henna. "It's from Damian. He wants to meet me at sundown."

"Damian? The ruler of the Fortis vampires?" Henna asked.

"No way. You're not meeting with vampires by yourself without Shane here. Not happening," Kara added.

"It doesn't necessarily say I have to come alone or anything, but I wonder what he wants?" Julianna asked softly.

"So, you think you'll meet him?" Emily asked.

"Yes. I'm curious what he wants." She turned to Kara. "Damian has never been very aggressive, but I would feel better if you came with me. As a human, I am more vulnerable to his powers."

"Of course, I'll come," Kara agreed confidently.

"I'll come too," Henna added. "Emily?"

Emily looked at her father, the broken man sitting on Kara's bed. She couldn't drop all this life-altering information on him and then leave him. "No, I'll stay here with my dad. But you three go, find out what Damian wants. Just don't agree to anything until

Shane is back."

"So, what do we do now?" Kara asked.

Julianna answered, clutching the note from Damian. What would a former vampire leader want with her? Was it because she was human now? Or because she was Shane's sister? Or did he simply regard her from her vampire life? "Now, we wait for sundown."

7

Shane stood up slowly. Other than Camilla, who was also trying to rise, the others Bianca had blown over stayed where they'd fallen, too tranced to move.

"So, what happens now?" Shane asked.

Bianca wiped Camilla's blood from her chin with her index finger and then licked it slowly. "I'll tell you the story and then you leave with your vampire friends. But the witch stays."

Camilla saw Shane tense up to argue, but she stopped him with a gentle hand on his shoulder. He could sense her again and she was confident that they should listen to Bianca. After all, isn't that why they'd come here?

"Deal." Shane narrowed his eyes and folded his arms across his chest.

"Not so high and mighty now, are you?" Bianca laughed. "You never considered that other vampires could do what you could do?" She sighed. "You are such a newborn."

"Tell me the story," Shane instructed. His patience was wearing thin. He wanted—no, needed—the information. But then he had to quickly spin his wheels on how to get them all out of there.

He wasn't leaving without Camilla.

A wicked grin danced across Bianca's lips. For a second she looked like she could almost be beautiful. "I had a sister. Beatrice. She was a seer. She's the one that foretold of the Dark Prophecy."

Bianca slithered toward Shane and Camilla. At least it felt like they might actually be close to useful information. Finally. "Go on," Shane urged.

"Beatrice was the good one. She loved humanity and hated killing. She would drink but only to satiate the burn. She always let her victims go. I thought that was weakness."

"What does this have to do with the prophecy?" Shane asked. He again fought the urge to strike Bianca and her game-playing.

"You remind me of her, dear Shane." Bianca hissed the words, words that were not hurtful but somehow came across as if they were meant to be insulting. "She couldn't always control what visions came to her, and toward the end, the Dark Prophecy consumed her thoughts. The blonde young man. Powerful, kind. *Newborn*." She spat the last word out like rotten food. "And she saw greatness in you, even as you ended our kind. Our beautiful species."

"I'm not eradicating vampires. I'm here to find out how to stop it," he argued with Bianca, even as she spoke in the past tense.

"Time is like a road. You only see where you are at the moment of your current journey. It doesn't mean that what's ahead doesn't exist, you just haven't arrived there yet." Bianca narrowed her eyes.

"Tell me how to change my course, then,"

Shane responded.

"You sleep with witches." She gestured at Camilla. "You allow humans to live with you." She leaned in very close to Shane. He could smell the coppery scent of Camilla's blood still swirling on her lips and tongue. "You are weak like Beatrice. You are weak because you are kind."

"So, you think I am too nice, like your sister. That I am too kind to humans. What is it you wanted me to know so that I can end the Dark Prophecy?" Shane kept his voice level, but the anger bubbled just under the surface.

"Your *kindness* is what led to Beatrice's undoing. And it will lead to yours." Bianca circled behind Shane. He followed her with his eyes, not trusting her, but still wanting to hear what she had to tell. "And it will lead to the end of the vampire species."

"That makes no sense," Shane stated.

"Does it not?" Bianca continued pacing around Shane and Camilla, and around Isabelle on the floor at his feet. "The village we lived in at the time of Beatrice's death was a quaint one. Small. In the mountains of Switzerland. You had to trust your neighbor because the town relied on bartering. We lived among them freely and my sister loved and trusted her townsfolk. But they began to suspect what we were. And one night a mob came after us, chanting for our heads." Bianca shrugged. "I thought the solution was simple. Kill them all, burn the village to the ground and move on. But Beatrice didn't want to hurt innocents, as she called them. She just wanted to run." Bianca stopped in front of Shane. "Weakness."

Camilla spoke, her voice soft but strong. "Kindness isn't weakness."

"Kindness has no place in the vampire world," Bianca spat venomously at Camilla. "We prey on humans. We need them to survive. At most they should be thought of as pets and playthings. But equals? To vampires?" Bianca threw her head back and laughed again, but this time it was malicious. This time the mere thought of something so ridiculous was angering her.

"What happened to the townspeople?" Shane asked. He wasn't sure why, but he felt that there was some connection to Beatrice and his own fate.

"I killed them. All. I did what needed to be done," Bianca shrugged.

"And Beatrice?" Camilla swallowed hard.

"Oh, I did what needed to be done there too," Bianca stated. She smiled, but it was mirthless. "I made sure she shared the fate of the townspeople. I killed her too."

"You killed your own sister?" Camilla asked, horrified, but also not entirely sure she'd understood correctly.

"I ended weakness," Bianca replied.

"So, I am weak like Beatrice, and yet you don't believe I can or will stop the prophecy," Shane stated. "What is it you think I need to know?"

"If you truly want to save vampires, you'll do what Beatrice could never do. Murder the witches in your compound,"—again she gestured at Camilla—

"and kill your abomination of a sister."

Shane pursed his lips in frustration, squeezing his fists to control his emotions. Bianca loved toying with her visitors, and he refused to give her what she wanted. "And if I don't?"

"If you refuse to do your duty as the leader of the united vampires, then I'll have to do what needs to be done." Bianca stood toe to toe with Shane, looking straight into his eyes. "And I'll have to eliminate your weakness, as I did Beatrice's."

"What exactly does that mean?" Camilla asked, but Shane already knew what Bianca had meant with her threat.

"My dear little witch, I'll have to kill him," she smiled. "To save the vampires, of course."

"How? How does my weakness lead to the end of the vampires?" Shane asked. He wasn't afraid to die, nor was he afraid to do the right thing for his species, but nothing was adding up.

Bianca slapped his cheek. "Your sister is just the first. Your kindness to her disgusting conversion will lead others to believe it's acceptable. This is how the plague will begin."

Shane thought about her words. "So either Julianna or I must die to save vampires?"

Bianca shrugged. "If it's even possible at all. As I said, your weakness has already led to the beginning of the end."

Shane thought about everything Bianca had said and wondered if there was truth in there. She was manipulative, murderous, and powerful, but she seemed to believe in what she said.

"Other vampires believed you might have solutions," Camilla stated, looking up at the old vampire with hard eyes that contrasted with Camilla's soft and gentle face. "But you're a washed up has-been who hides out in caves. You claim Shane is the weak one? Bullshit. The only weak vampire I see in this room is *you*. You're the one who is afraid of the prophecy."

Bianca's face contorted in anger at Camilla's words. She pulled her arms back and pushed Camilla against the cave wall with a powerful burst of air.

But Camilla didn't let it faze her. "Now, Shane!" she shouted, shaking him from his thoughts and debates about the validity of anything Bianca had said.

The plan now was simple. Save Camilla and get everyone out of Bianca's cave. Shane built up a fireball and threw it at the old, tattered vampire. She screamed as she burned, but it didn't stop her from flinging a force of air at Shane.

But he was able to create a force of air of his own and push it back on Bianca's. They shoved invisible air at each other, while Bianca continued to burn, for several seconds. Clearly Bianca couldn't summon water, or she would've put herself out by now.

Bianca stopped first, pulling back her air and then rolling, putting out the flames as she did so, behind her makeshift throne. Shane lifted it with ease, tossing the stones to a far corner in the back of the darkened cave. Bianca cowered before him, charred and melted. She looked like a waking nightmare.

While Shane focused on Bianca, Camilla ran to Isabelle and Luke and guided them to Elias. Bianca's trance on them seemed to be abating as she fought with Shane, because they slowly began to wake and come to their senses. They watched, struggling to catch up to the scene before them as Shane used air to force Bianca back against a cave wall, slamming her charred body. But before she hit, she had the wherewithal to send a force of her own that sent Shane sliding back to where Camilla had been pinned moments ago.

Isabelle tensed, preparing to run into the battle, but Camilla stopped her. "Not yet."

From her pocket, Camilla pulled out a small hex bag and handed it to Isabelle. "Get close enough to put this on her body."

Bianca stood, her melted hair and blackened body not much more than a skeleton by now. She would regenerate with blood and time to heal, but for now she looked as close to death as a vampire could be.

She stormed toward Shane, tossing him with ease with her powers. And Shane let her.

He used himself as the distraction so Isabelle could get close. Sneaking up from behind she shoved the hex bag into the melted clothes that dripped from Bianca's body. Noticing the new foe, she tossed Isabelle back across the room.

"Fire, Shane," Camilla instructed. And he obeyed, sending a small handful of fire right to the hex bag. As it lit, Bianca froze right where she was, unable to move.

Isabelle ran up behind her and ripped Bianca's arms off. The black stubs dripped little blood as she tossed them to the ground. Shane slowly walked over.

"Today, I am going to do you a great kindness, even if it *is* weakness," Shane said as he walked toward Bianca where she remained a charred statue. "Today I am going to end your infernal existence and minimize your suffering." He nodded at Isabelle and the warrior took great glee in ripping Bianca's head from her charred body. She was so burnt that it pulled off easily.

From the spell that had been cast, her crispy shell of a body remained frozen where it stood. Isabelle threw the head so it ricocheted off the wall.

"What a bitch," Isabelle announced as Bianca's crusty head bounced on the floor.

Luke shook his head, continuing to clear it from Bianca's trance. He looked at the scene before him and asked, "What the hell just happened?"

Shane walked to Camilla and kissed her forehead. "You scared me to death, but I know why you did what you did." To Luke he answered, "I got what I needed from Bianca."

"Is that her?" Elias pointed at the black statue in the middle of the cave.

"It was." Isabelle folded her arms across her chest and let a victory smile creep across her face.

"And you're in big trouble for sneaking off like that, Isabelle." Shane pointed at her.

"Please," Isabelle snorted. "What would you have done? Thrown her around to death? You need me for the dirty work."

Shane smiled in spite of himself. He wanted to stay mad at her for endangering both her and Camilla's lives, but her attitude always kept him from staying angry.   If Bianca hadn't possessed advanced mind control, his money would've been on Isabelle every day of the week.

"So what now, my Lord?" Elias asked.

"Now," Shane looked around at his team. They were family to him now. They meant everything to him. He knew he couldn't let the prophecy come to pass. He couldn't let them all die. "Now we go back and end the Dark Prophecy."

"What do we do with Bianca's feeders?" Camilla pointed at the few humans who were chained, but still alive, around the room.

"We let them go and then destroy the cave," Shane instructed. "Camilla will transport us back."

"Letting the humans live." Camilla smiled at Shane.   "Compassion for humans is what Bianca thought would be your undoing."

"Bianca was brainwashed by the years she

spent fermenting in her own evil," Shane responded. "And you were right. Hiding in a cave for centuries? She exposed her own cowardice."

He tucked a lock of hair behind Camilla's ear, thankful that no serious harm had come to her, despite the puncture wounds on her neck.

"Did she actually have anything useful to say?" Luke asked. "Cuz all I remember was a warm feeling and then I was off imagining myself as Bianca's love slave. And I liked it."

Elias coughed uncomfortably. "I had weird thoughts too."

Isabelle smiled. "Me too."

Shane put a possessive arm around Camilla as he explained. "Bianca was a powerful vampire. She was able to put all of you in a trance. And it was her sister who foretold the prophecy, so she did know a few details. But her perceptions were twisted by her own malice."

He walked over to the first human, weak from loss of blood and likely starvation. He shot a laser of fire from his hand and melted the chains that bound the slave to the cave wall. "But I won't let anything happen to my friends and family. What Bianca thought was weakness, I'm going to use as strength."

"You know I think of you like a brother, Shane," Luke sighed and leaned against the cave wall, "but since you resurrected, I feel like the life of a vampire has gotten a lot more complicated."

Shane continued releasing humans, who stumbled weakly and blindly in the dark cave. It was clear they wouldn't be able to make it very far on their own.

He turned to Camilla. "Are you able to transport them to a hospital?"

Camilla smiled. "Of course."

"You can thank me for that," Isabelle gloated. "I helped her find the ingredient she needed for transportation spells."

Like a big brother, Shane walked over to Isabelle and rubbed her head. "I am very thankful for you, Isabelle."

"There's just one thing I don't understand," Elias stated. "How exactly are we going to stop the prophecy with kindness?"

8

"This is too important." Damian continued pacing across his cabin floor. Notch sat listening to him, his legs crossed as he leaned back against the couch. "No matter the risk, I have to do this."

"You'd better be certain," Notch responded in a blasé tone, a glance at a rogue hangnail distracting him. "I wouldn't want to risk angering the chosen one."

"I know. It's hard to explain." Damian sat in an armchair, overdramatically flopping his arms down as he did so. "I just feel it in my bones. It won't be right for some..."

Notch looked up at his former tribe leader. "It won't be right for anyone."

Damian acquiesced. "Others won't understand.

But it's what *I* need to do."

Notch leaned forward, resting his elbows on his knees. "You know how I feel. I think you are being rash and emotional. And if you regret your actions, there may be no coming back from that."

Damian leaned forward too, clasping Notch's hands in his. "I know. I'll be careful that none of this blows back on you."

Notch pulled away. "I don't care about that." He was slightly offended that Damian thought his hesitance was based on self-preservation. He stared at Damian's face—a face he knew so well. He'd loved this man for centuries. But for the first time, he saw past the carefree façade of someone who only cared about parties and lasciviousness. Damian looked tired. Haggard. Done.

And wasn't part of loving someone supporting them even if you didn't completely agree with their decisions?

"I am aware of the ire I may cause in Shane." Damian looked at the ground. "I've thought about that a lot. He's given me a certain amount of peace in his short reign. And I'll forever be grateful for that." He glanced back up at Notch's discerning expression. "But sometimes you have to look beyond the short term and see the bigger picture."

Notch understood that. He knew the years of trying to run the Fortis compound had taken their toll. Damian had enjoyed the power it granted, but not the weight of the burden that leadership carried. You couldn't please everyone. Vampires were often angry. Sometimes vampires even lost their lives. The Shadow Wars had been a constant stress and ever-present promise of conflict and battles for centuries.

"Do you remember the day we met?" Notch asked out of the blue.

Damian smiled at the memory. "Of course. How could I forget?"

"Isabelle introduced us. She thought you might like to have a music man in the tribe." Notch laughed at Isabelle recruiting a tribeless vampire to the Fortis compound so that Damian could throw better parties.

Damian shook his head, remembering the day Notch had stepped into their lives. "Isabelle and I may not have always seen eye to eye, but she did understand me." He missed his former number two, even though he knew she was running in circles that fit her personality better. She would always want to be where the action was. Damian always wanted to be where the action *wasn't*.

"Perhaps you should talk to Izzy?" Notch suggested. "She's friends with Julianna, too."

Damian fervently shook his head. "It's better that fewer people know about my plans. Word will spread quickly once the deed is done."

"Then I'll go with you tonight when you meet with Shane's sister," Notch announced.

Damian shook his head. "I can't ask that of you. Don't get involved."

Notch stood. It was almost sundown anyway. "You didn't ask. I volunteered. And I'm not letting you do something as huge as this on your own."

Damian stared long and hard at his best friend.

Was this the beginning of the end? It sure felt like it. He rubbed his hands on his knees and then stood next to Notch. "Okay."

Damian reached for Notch's hand, but Notch surprised him by pulling him into a strong hug. Damian might not have been much of a fighter, but he'd protected his tribe and family for many years. And now he was risking it all.

9

"Why do we always have to go to spooky woods to have meeting places?" Julianna asked aloud as they trudged through a dense forest of trees high into the mountains not too far from the former Fortis compound. The moon hung low in the sky, casting a soft glow of light and making the sky seem more dark blue than black. Stars were beginning to peek through, popping up here and there and decorating the background above them.

"What on earth could be spookier in these woods than the creatures you are marching up with and the creatures you are planning to meet?" Kara asked, purposefully keeping her steps slow so she didn't leave the witches and the human in the dust.

"I might be a witch, but I'm not a 'creature'," Henna took exception to Kara's choice of words.

"I just see the world a bit differently now as a human," Julianna explained, as she stepped to avoid a large tree branch blocking her path. "I still remember my life as a vampire, but it's murky, like a dream. I feel vulnerable now. And the night seems... menacing."

Kara laughed. "You *are* vulnerable now."

"What do you think he wants?" Henna asked the question they'd been circling back to since Julianna had first received the note.

"All I can figure is it has something do with Dimas. It always seems like everything keeps coming back to him." Julianna's shoulders slumped a bit at the memory of her trust and belief in him. The Betrayer. She was ashamed at her poor choice in judgment. Luke and Shane had seen right through him, but she had fought for him.

She had *died* for him.

He had betrayed them all, but the personal betrayal stung deep in her heart. A tiny sliver of pain and hurt that didn't feel like it could ever heal. And her human heart amplified the pain, echoing through her soul and preventing her from forgetting no matter how she may try.

"I see him," Kara announced. With her vampire sight she could see the best of the three of them, so even though Julianna couldn't see what Kara saw, she believed her. "He's standing in a clearing just ahead. And he's not alone."

For just a moment's hesitation, Julianna froze at Kara's words, wondering who was there with Damian, worried it might be an ambush. But she'd made the decision to come, and she hoped her bodyguards would be enough.

She had no idea what they were stumbling toward.

They trudged on in silence, only the sound of twigs and leaves crunching beneath their feet slicing through the night air. For all three of them, curiosity beat out worry.

Kara thought about Isabelle. It was strange

that, as a vampire, she felt closer to Isabelle than she did to her own sister. Knowing she might be going into battle forced her to stand a bit taller. And tell herself that she would do whatever necessary to make Isabelle proud. She didn't want to hurt Emily, but it was Isabelle who inspired her in this moment.

Just beyond the edge of trees, two figures stood in the moonlight. In a clearing, as Kara had described. Before Julianna could pull the branch up and out of their way, Henna placed a hand on Julianna's shoulder.

"We're with you, sister," Henna whispered. Damian could likely hear it anyway, Julianna knew, but knowing that she was backed by both the coven and the vampires she lived with did provide her human heart some comfort. She stepped into the clearing to face the unknown.

Damian smiled when he saw her. As she neared him, she recognized Notch who had often been at Damian's side when Isabelle wasn't. As a vampire, Julianna had known these two well. Fought them often under Dimas.

"You came." The relief in Damian's voice was evident. He made no pretense to mask it.

Julianna nodded slightly before starting the preamble she'd been preparing. "Just so you know, my memories of my vampire life are hazy. If there are details you need from my time under Dimas, I can't promise I can provide them."

Damian shook his head. "No. Dimas can rot in hell for all I care."

Julianna relaxed a little in his dismissal of Dimas, but Kara tensed at his somewhat aggressive tone.

"The witch and I are here for her protection, so don't try anything," Kara announced through elongated fangs.

Damian held his hands up in submission. "No, I just want to talk."

Julianna believed him, so she gestured for Kara to stand down. Henna, true to her nature, stood silently observing, like a beautiful lioness in wait.

Damian shifted uncomfortably, like he was

embarrassed to ask what he wanted to know. But after a moment of awkward silence he said, "I want to know how you became human again."

"Oh." Julianna was truly taken aback at this. It hadn't been an option in any of her thoughts about what he might want. She looked at Henna, who nodded in support that she should answer. Julianna licked her lips as she remembered the day it happened. "I was murdered by Dimas, as you know. But the witches resurrected me using their spells and their own blood. When I came back to life, I was human, not vampire. I don't know why."

Damian watched her carefully, searching her face for the truth in her story. He didn't look skeptical, or even shocked. Most likely he had heard the rumors already. Vampires were a gossipy bunch. That much Julianna remembered well.

Damian looked back at Notch, who nodded his support just as Henna had done for Julianna.

Damian, summoning courage, asked, "Do you think it could be done again?"

"I have no idea," Julianna answered honestly.

"What exactly are you asking?" Kara got straight to the point.

Damian didn't respond right away, and everyone waited wordlessly. Kara might've been blunt, but all three ladies wanted to hear the answer. They all let the silence drag on and become heavy with anticipation.

"I want to be human again too," Damian finally said. He had dragged them all out here in the middle of the night for this very conversation, so he had no idea why he had been struggling to form the words. It was time. Time to find out if this were actually an option.

It was Kara that voiced the shock at his response. "You *want* to be a human again? Like no longer a vampire?"

"Necromancy is dangerous. It takes a piece of us witches for it to happen. You'd be asking for a huge sacrifice," Henna added to Kara's outburst.

Damian said nothing. He wasn't sure how to articulate his dream. But Julianna understood. She was the only one who possibly could. No one asked you if you wanted to become a vampire. You just wake from the dead one day craving blood. And once she was human again, she knew fervently that she wanted to stay that way.

Damian didn't want to be a monster anymore.

Julianna gently grabbed Damian's hands in her own. He startled a bit at the gentle touch. "What do you remember of your old human life?"

Damian shook his head slowly, somberly. "Very little." For Damian, centuries had passed in vampire form. The memories would have faded and blown away slowly with the passage of time.

"So, you really just want to have a choice in what you are, don't you?" Julianna asked.

Behind her, Kara snorted. "Why would anyone choose to be the hunted rather than the hunter?"

Julianna snapped her head back to Kara before anyone could answer. "I did." Julianna looked back to Damian. She could see how tired he was. Perhaps his soul had been at war with itself throughout the

Shadow Wars. He had always had the reputation as more of lover than a fighter. He wasn't overtly cruel or manipulative, like Regina. He wasn't evil like Dimas. Maybe he'd always struggled to be the vampire that the vampire world expected him to be. "Dimas wanted to turn me back into a vampire," Julianna continued, "and I fought him. I wanted to remain a human. So I understand wanting to choose not to be a creature of the night."

Damian lifted his chin, hope daring to brim inside his eyes. "So you can walk in the sun again?"

Julianna smiled. "I can." She rubbed her throat. "And the controlling burn is gone."

Kara, still incredulous, whispered, "But you'd be so fragile."

Damian didn't have an answer to that. He felt fragile even as a vampire. But Julianna spoke for the both of them.

"No. Being human is powerful. Maybe not like Shane powerful, or vampire speed powerful. But in the ways that truly matter like kindness and love and forgiveness."

"That makes no sense," Kara responded.

Henna folded her arms and leaned on one hip. "Even assuming it all made sense that Damian would want to become human again, where are you going to find a coven willing? It takes a lot out of us."

Damian hung his head. He hadn't known it was reliant on witches.   What little hope he'd felt was waning.

Julianna lifted his chin gently, so she could look directly into his eyes. "Is this truly what you want?"

Damian nodded. "It is."

Notch spoke up. "Even if he was a human, I'd take care of him just as Shane cares for you. He would never be alone."

Julianna squeezed Damian's hands. "Then I'll find a way to help you, Damian. If this is what you want, then we'll make it happen."

"This is crazy," Kara said. Her eyes were wild, as if they were plotting a heinous crime. And perhaps in her mind, this was a crime. After all, Damian would have to die before he was resurrected. Again.

"It's not as crazy as it sounds," Julianna said, shaking her head. She had no idea how to make someone understand, but she felt the need to try, for Damian's sake if not her own. "It's obviously possible. Look at me. If we did it once, we could do it again."

"It's a risk, for sure," Henna stated. She was less confident that they *could* do it again. She didn't want to voice it, but they'd had Theresa the last time. And Theresa was gone. One small change in a spell can make a big difference.

"I've always been different, everyone knows that," Damian explained. "And I didn't know why. I just felt it. But when I heard what happened to you, Julianna, I *knew*. I'm too human to be a good vampire. And if I have a chance to be what feels right, why wouldn't I take that chance? I'm tired of feeling this way."

"I understand," Julianna answered. And she did. Probably the only one standing in the clearing under a canopy of moonlight who did. "I'll have to talk to Shane. We can't plan something as big as this without him. And possibly Camilla."

"But only tell who you must," Notch stated. "I worry about this getting out of hand."

"Are you worried they might kill him before he's ready to die?" Kara said sarcastically.

"It would cause fear and panic," Julianna answered for Notch. She knew vampires and their politics. They'd feel their world unraveling and who knows what that would lead to?

"Julianna." Damian met her eyes. She watched him carefully. In that moment he did look fragile. Human. And she felt a kindred spirit in a sea of creatures. "I'm ready, so I'm trusting you with this. Do what you have to do."

"I respect your choice," Julianna responded. "And I promise to do what I can to help you. Without telling the whole vampire world."

And Damian surprised her by yanking her and pulling her into a strong embrace. Kara hissed and let her claws extend, prepared to kill him if it was a trap after all and he tried anything on Julianna.

But instead, she saw Julianna wrap her arms around the fragile vampire's back and squeeze him in return.

Kara looked at Henna, who was smiling, and let her claws retract. "Humans. Such saps." But there was no malice in her voice.

And they let Damian and Julianna embrace, both understanding the other in a way no one else could. Both feeling whole by the simple act of hugging. A little sliver of humanity in the dark, oppressive night.

10

"It was a fool's errand," Shane announced to his vampire council. "Bianca had gone crazy after all the centuries stewing in her own evil."

"So you learned nothing." Johann leaned in, a crease across his brow expressing his surprise at the turn of events. After all, he'd been the one to suggest Bianca might be a source of information. His hair was slicked back in a low ponytail and he wore a long coat, denoting an old aristocrat.

Shane shrugged. "I suppose it depends on whether or not you want to believe what she said. I'm not sure I do."

Isabelle added, somewhat in awe, "She was very powerful."

Camilla added. "And evil. And manipulative. Did you know she murdered her own sister?"

Johann looked down at his hands. "It has long been rumored."

"She murdered her for being too nice. And she said kindness is what leads the prophecy to fruition. It's a tough one to buy." Shane leaned back, resting one foot on his knee. His hair was getting longer and his blonde curls were framing his face.

"Yeah, yeah. She's evil. She hates kindness. Hardly an epiphany. We're vampires." Regina glanced at her nails from where she sat on Alexi's lap. "What did you learn about the prophecy? You must have learned something?"

Shane stared at Regina for a moment before speaking in a low voice. "She said there's no way to stop it. If Beatrice saw it, then it had already come true."

Regina stood, panic on her face. The vampires expressed denial and shock to one another. All except Damian, who looked at Julianna in the back of the room. Julianna grabbed his hands gently. Most people didn't notice the two in the back who didn't seem to care about the prophecy anymore, but the intimate act was caught by Luke. The jealous monster within threatened to break through the surface, but he swallowed it down.

"If there's no way to stop it, then we are already doomed," Regina announced. She wore a low-cut red dress and tall black stiletto heels. Shane knew as sexy as she looked, she could also snap someone in two if she wanted to. "Pardon me, but I don't want to spend another minute of my final undead days in a basement with you assholes. I'm going to get my kicks."

She sashayed her hips toward the door, stopping briefly to whisper in Luke's ear, "Come by later, handsome."

Alexi was right behind her. The room was still as they waited for the door to slam behind them.

"Does this mean you don't believe Bianca?" Johann asked. He was still calm and reserved, like

Shane was. The room was buzzing with nervous energy, but somehow these two rose above it.

"I do not," Shane announced.

"But the first part came true," Isabelle stated. "Dimas tried to stop it and it still came true."

"I believe we are masters of our own fates. Vampires wanted an end to the Shadow Wars, so it was easy for me to step into the role *you* gave me," Shane stated, his head held high. It was easy to forget he was still really just a newborn. "But we don't want the second part, so we fight it. If it hasn't happened yet, it can still be stopped."

"So what's the plan?" Luke asked, Elias sitting silently by his side. Elias remained focused on Shane, but Shane watched Luke's eyes bounce between Julianna, sitting close to Damian, and Shane.

"First, we have to know what we are dealing with." Shane turned his attention fully to Elias. "I need twenty scouts all throughout the vampire territory, reporting back on any disease or plague they see."

Elias stood, nodding his head in

acknowledgment. "It will be done."

"We don't know when or where the eradication could begin. We might need scouts for centuries," Shane added.

"I can set up shifts," Elias responded.

Johann stood. "I can also ask my compound to stay alert to rumors."

Shane stood and shook both their hands. "Once we know, we can finalize the plan. If it's disease, we can quarantine. If it's violence, we can fight."

"And if it's witchcraft?" Luke raised an eyebrow and dared to glance at Camilla. Camilla glowered back in response.

"When we understand the threat, we can neutralize it," Shane responded, no hesitance in his voice. Whatever the threat might be, he knew it wasn't coming from Camilla.

"Then we have our orders." Elias did a slight bow and exited through the back door. Johann followed, his promise to support Shane his parting words. Only Damian rose and left without a word.

A heavy silence lingered in the air after the other council members had left, leaving Shane, Isabelle, Luke, Camilla and Julianna staring at one another in the basement. Julianna rose to come closer to the group from where she'd been sitting with Damian, but Isabelle held up a hand.

"Please don't come any closer. You smell like a delicious snack." Isabelle breathed deeply and then looked away. Julianna sat again in the back corner.

"But I don't?" Camilla turned to Isabelle. They were on the same couch and she was still human.

Isabelle crinkled her nose. "No, I can smell your witchiness."

Shane stood and walked over to the cabinet where Dimas had kept all his liquor. He raised a bottle toward the group. "Anyone?"

"Why not? Let's toast the end of our race," Luke responded.

"You don't know that," Isabelle snapped.

"Izz. I never even believed in the dumb ole prophecy. Some old hag from Europe claimed to see the coming of the vampire Christ and then the world ends?   Nonsense."   Luke held his hands up questioningly.   "Except...things are starting to come true. And you can't pick and choose which parts you believe. If you believe the prophecy, you believe the end is coming."

"Maybe she was wrong?" Shane proposed as he handed a drink to Luke.

Luke looked up at Shane as he grabbed the drink. "She hasn't been yet." And he swallowed the contents of the glass in one gulp.

"Well, what I'm saying is, maybe she misinterpreted what she saw. It's easier than you think to sense something and see a glimpse and jump to a conclusion. Maybe what she saw *will* come true, but what if it's not what she thought it was?" Shane sat back in his seat at the front of the room. He dangled his glass over the armrest, shaking the liquid with a gentle rotation of his wrist.

"So she saw vampires dropping dead and somehow misconstrued that?" Luke shook his head.

"Shane is right," Julianna voiced from her corner. She looked so sweet and pure. Luke wondered how she could possibly become more beautiful simply by shedding her vampire traits. "We don't know enough to jump to conclusions."

Even as he stood, Luke knew he was being an idiot. But he couldn't help it. She had been sitting so close to Damian. He walked toward her and with no decorum whatsoever he asked at full volume, "So what's with you and Damian all of a sudden?"

Julianna glanced at Shane, but he looked just as curious. No one in this room knew what Damian had asked of her. "It's not what you think."

"Then what is it? Because it looked like the two of you were going to hook up later," Luke accused. He hated himself for acting like a jealous boyfriend, but, dammit, he felt like a jealous boyfriend.

Julianna stood. She had wanted to have a private conversation with Shane. "It's not something I want everyone to hear."

"So you are in love with him?" Luke asked,

shock overwhelming the jealousy for a moment.

Julianna shoved Luke's chest and rolled her eyes. Of course, with her human strength now, Luke barely felt it. "No, you jackass. He wants to be human." She blurted it out, but then sighed with relief once it was out there. Without the truth, the whole room seemed to be coming to its own conclusions. Better to just make it known.

The vampires and Camilla all just stared at her for a moment before Luke howled with laughter. He had to press his hands to his eyes to stop them from tearing up as he laughed harder and harder.

"Why is that funny?" Julianna demanded, but her question only made Luke laugh more.

"Damian is the world's biggest loser," Isabelle responded.

Camilla played with her ponytail. "He thinks that your freak incident is something we can just replicate on demand?"

Luke, out of breath from laughing so hard, added, "Why would anyone stop being strong and powerful to become human again?"

Julianna raised hurt eyes to Luke. She wanted to shout and make them all understand. But they wouldn't, and she would only get emotional as humans often did, and it would all backfire. So she did the only other thing she could think to do at that moment. She ran from the room, fighting back the tears.

Watching her go, Luke asked, "Was it something I said?"

"*She's* human, dumbass." Isabelle rolled her eyes.

"But it wasn't something she chose. It just happened to her. I better go talk to her." Luke started to follow Julianna's path when Shane grabbed his arm.

"I just had a vision," Shane said. His voice was flat and robotic, whether from the shock or from being in some sort of trance state, no one knew. "It isn't me who brings the beginning of the end."

Shane looked at Luke but said nothing more, so Luke asked, "That's good, right?"

Shane shook his head. "Julianna is the one we

have to stop."

Everyone froze at Shane's words. They believed him, they always had. But they had to process his words, to struggle and find meaning in exactly what he was saying to them. Only Isabelle had the wits about her to respond in any meaningful way.

"Well, shit," she said, speaking for the whole group.

11

"Dad, Shane is back. You should meet him." Emily spoke to her father, who was still sitting on Kara's bed. He hadn't moved or said much in the past twenty-four hours. And Emily had scarcely left his side.

She saw a man who had had it all. He'd been living the good life, the stuff dreams are made of. And then the rug was pulled out from under him. Life had thrown him some tough curveballs. No, not life, Emily thought. *Theresa.*

Even as a witch there was only so much Emily could do to get him back on track. For a fleeting second, she wished Theresa were alive again so her father could smack her.

"Is he a vampire?" At least her father was forming coherent sentences. He appeared to be more lucid. Emily took that as a good sign.

"He is, but...he's not what you'd imagine. He sees the good in all creatures," Emily explained. She sat next to her father on the bed.

"Does he drink blood?" Richard asked with wide eyes.

"Well, yes of course, but..."

"Then I'll pass," Richard cut her off. Beyond Kara, he wasn't ready for vampires. Even Kara he wasn't ready for. "Where's the pretty blonde normal one?"

"Julianna? I'm sure she's in the compound somewhere," Emily reasoned. She didn't actually know, but Julianna, Kara and Henna had all come home from meeting with Damian in the middle of the night. And she knew Julianna had joined the vampire council early this morning. Most likely she was nearby.

"I only trust you and Julianna," Richard stated.

If he was going to be nervous around witches

and vampires, he couldn't stay long in the compound. "I can take you home as soon as you feel up to it."

"I'm not sure I can go back to that place. I have no idea which memories are real and which are manufactured." Richard shook his head. His shoulders slumped forward. The weight of all that Theresa had done to him was taking its toll both mentally and physically. "I'll have to sell that house."

Emily nodded. She would be sad to see her childhood home sold to another family, but she wasn't sure she could go back either. And Kara probably never would. Everything had changed.

"What a night, let me tell you." Kara burst through her bedroom door with very little regard for the humans on the other side of it. "I'll save you some of the gory details, Dad, but let me just say I am a damn good hunter." She smiled ruefully, eyebrows raised.

Sensing a need to keep this conversation away from Kara's nighttime excursions, Emily asked, "What did Damian want?"

"Oh yeah," Kara answered, like it was such old

news she almost forgot it was worth mentioning. "He wants to be human like Julianna. Kill him. Resurrect him. Hope he comes back human like she did." She shook her head. "He's nuts."

Emily stood. She was so shocked by what she was hearing that she couldn't stay still. "What? And what did Julianna say?"

Kara shrugged. "She said she'd talk to Shane. I don't know what's happening in this world when vampires want to be humans. What's next? Lions choosing to become gazelles?"

"But that's it, Kara. Don't you see?" Richard stood, energy and hope dawning on his face for the first time in a while. "You could be human again and we can all go back home together."

"Dad." Kara leaned on one hip. "I'd have to *die*. Again. And it's only been done once. We don't even know if it can happen again."

"And it all depends on Shane. He's the most powerful vampire ever to walk this earth. He could stop this dream before it ever gets off the ground."

Emily looked between her father, hope still brimming in his eyes, and her sister, who stood defiantly. Emily knew Kara loved being a vampire. But it wouldn't matter anyway if it were just a foolish notion.

"Then take me to him." Richard stood up tall.

"Are you sure?" Emily asked. Just a few moments ago he was too afraid to leave the room.

"Yes. I'm ready. I'm ready to meet Shane, the all-powerful vampire who likes all creatures," Richard answered.

"Except Theresa." Kara smiled. "He *hated* Theresa."

"Good. Then we have something in common," Richard responded.

"What exactly are you going to say to him, Dad? That you want him to let Damian be a test subject so, in case it works, I can turn back too?" Kara asked.

Richard looked at Kara's face, so similar and yet so different in its vampire form. How had all of this gotten so far out of control? "Well, yes. Basically."

Kara shook her head. "This is way bigger than

you and me, Dad. It's just not that simple."

"Just be honest, Kara, you don't want to turn back," Emily added. She wanted the conversation to at least be an honest one. They were family, after all.

"Don't put words in my mouth, Emily." Kara started to get angry.

"You like being a vampire, Kara. Don't get Dad's hopes up for nothing!"

As Kara got angrier, her fangs elongated. It was subconscious, just something that a vampire's body did uncontrollably. She stepped in front of her sister and said, "Stay out of this!" and she shoved her. Emily's body flew back, hitting the wall with a thud.

Richard recoiled, physically withdrew, horrified at the monster before him. Kara froze, shocked at how easily she had thrown Emily, and watched her dad cower in the corner. Emily shook her head, dazed. She wasn't seriously hurt and the rejuvenation potion would keep her from staying hurt for long anyway. Emily stood up and went to her father.

Kara ran from the room at vampire speed. The gust of wind from her departure blowing the door against the wall behind her.

"Dad, it's okay. I'm okay," Emily explained to her father, opening her arms in front of him to show him just how okay she was. She didn't want this to scare him off. She didn't want to lose him again.

Richard's eyes stayed locked on the door where Kara had just exited. His eyes were still wide with shock. Through gritted teeth, he said, "Take me to Shane. Now."

Emily nodded and took her father gently by the arm to lead him to Shane. They needed to meet at some point—she couldn't just have a random human in the compound without Shane knowing—so she figured now was as good a time as any. She just hoped bringing him into a den of vampires wasn't going to backfire egregiously.

12

There was a soft rap on Julianna's door. She wanted to tell whoever was there to go away, but curiosity and manners got the best of her and instead she called, "Come in."

Shane peeked his blonde head in, watching his sister with eyes so much like her own. His eyes reminded her of a simpler life. Running through the valley as carefree kids. Riding bikes in the street. Playing in a park. Shane's eyes reminded her of home.

"Hey," he said by way of greeting. He walked over to the bed where she was sitting up, under the covers, and sat down next to her. "Thank you for taking Henna and Kara with you. To meet Damian. I mean, Kara is a bit young, but I'm glad you didn't go alone."

Of course, he knew. He looked so much like the kid brother she had always protected, it was easy to forget that he didn't need her anymore. Hell, it was she who needed his protection now.

"Damian is harmless," Julianna answered. She knew she'd been taking a risk when she'd gone, but now that it was over and no harm had come to any of them, the worry had been senseless. No reason to go on about it.

Shane nodded once, but then he moved on. "Did he tell you why he wanted to turn back?"

"He said he never felt like he fit in."

"Do you believe him?"

Julianna sighed. "I know if someone doesn't want to be a monster anymore, I don't see why the whole world has to care. Who else gets harmed if Damian makes this choice and the witches agree? Even if it doesn't work, only Damian dies."

Shane looked away. He wanted to handle this delicately. For all his power and ability to control the elements, he had no trick up his sleeve for breaking bad news. And no vampire that he knew had ever wanted to keep a relationship with his human sister before, so there was no precedent for any of this. "What if I told you, Damian is the beginning of the end?"

Julianna looked at his face. Shane was many things, but overly dramatic wasn't one of them. She knew he was a great leader because he cared, truly cared, about his family. Humans, vampires, witches. All of them had a place in this home. "How can that be true?"

"I had a vision, Jules." Shane looked right up and locked eyes with his sister. "The ritual with Damian will work. And then others will follow, by choice in the beginning. But the curse will spread and others will transform without their consent. And vampires will be eradicated, just as the Dark Prophecy foretold."

He didn't appear to be teasing her, but his story didn't make sense. "That's ridiculous." But she didn't sound convincing, even to herself. She had *always* believed in the prophecy. It was hard to start questioning things now. But her human mind processed things slightly differently. "Turning human isn't a curse, Shane."

But before Shane could retort with the vampire perspective, the bedroom door opened unceremoniously and Luke swept in. And even though she was mad at him and annoyed at his inability to knock, Julianna couldn't help but stare at his perfectly formed face and tall, muscular build. He even had the decency to look a little contrite.

"Am I interrupting anything?" Luke asked, although then he walked all the way in and joined them on the bed, regardless of the answer.

Julianna rolled her eyes, forcing herself to stay mad, even as her heart softened.

"I was explaining to Julianna why she can't help Damian," Shane explained.

"Yeah, about that..." Luke looked at Julianna, and she looked away. She didn't want him to see her being emotional. She didn't want him to know she was succumbing to his charms. Shane may be powerful, but Luke had his own methods. His ability to make a woman get weak in the knees was just as effective at getting his way as Shane and his fireballs. He lifted her chin gently with his finger and forced her to look in his eyes. Julianna was struck by the fact he and Shane both could easily compel her—force her to stay in her room and never help Damian. But they didn't. They were reasoning with her and somehow that felt respectful. She allowed Luke the benefit of hearing him out. "I didn't mean to call you weak. It's different with Damian. He's supposed to be leading vampires. You're...well, you're you. Anyway, I'm sorry."

"You guys just don't get it. Neither of you do." Julianna pulled her knees up to her chin and wrapped her arms around her legs. "Imagine if you could've lived out the rest of your human days. Enjoying the sun, food, family. Knowing you're immortal makes all those things more precious. We may not be able to run fast or throw people, but we're not weak. Our mortal life *is* our strength."

Luke wrinkled his nose. "Yeah. I still don't get it."

Shane rested a hand gently on his sister's knee. "I think it's amazing that you get a second chance at being human. I really do. But I am the leader of vampires. And I'm pretty sure that doesn't mean I should participate in an event that will end the species."

"But you said some vampires would do it willingly? So some actually agree with Damian?" Julianna argued. She wasn't sure why she should help Damian, really. Her brother was her brother. These people were her family. Luke had become a partner and best friend. But something about Damian's plight—and the fact no one on earth could understand choosing being a human over vampire but her—connected her to him in a way she couldn't explain. Or fight.

Shane narrowed his eyes. He wanted her to see reason. "If you help Damian, you destroy vampires,

Jules."

"It's not destruction if they want it, Shane," Julianna answered back.

"Wait." Luke looked from Julianna to Shane and then back at Julianna. "Some vampires want to copy Damian?"

"Yes, that's how the end begins. Damian's transformation will start a movement," Shane explained to his best friend.

Luke ran his fingers through his hair. "Whoa. A movement? To be human again?" He stood up from the bed and pointed at Shane. "And you saw this? In your vision?"

Shane nodded. "I did."

Luke started pacing. "If you saw it, then it's coming true. This is all happening. We're done. Gone."

Shane raised an eyebrow. "I thought you didn't believe in the prophecy."

"I didn't. Don't." Luke stopped for a second and turned to Shane. "But you saw it. Beatrice saw it. Two powerful seers. I don't like these odds."

Shane rose to meet Luke's eyes. "Do you believe in me?"

"Of course."

"I'm going to stop it."

Without getting up, Julianna spoke to the most important men in her life. "What if you shouldn't?"

But before Shane could ask Julianna more on that, the bedroom door opened without preamble yet again.

"I tried to stop them," Camilla explained, following behind Emily and her father.

Julianna flopped her arms. These were the moments she wished she was a vampire, so she could toss them all out on their butts. "Why doesn't the whole compound come in and we can make this a giant party?"

"I'm sorry, Shane, but my father really wanted to meet you. And I wanted you to know I had brought him here," Emily explained.

"I knew," Shane answered. He remained stoic. "I just had to deal with some other pressing matters."

"Sir, I'm Richard." Emily's father extended a hand. Shane stared at it for a long moment and then shook it. It was such a human gesture. One he hadn't done in what felt like forever. "I don't plan to stay for long. I just had to detox from Theresa's magic. Or so I'm told."

"It's true," Shane nodded solemnly. "And you are welcome to stay as long as you like. Emily and Kara are part of this family. So you are too, now."

"Ah, for fucks sake, Shane." Luke rolled his eyes dramatically. "If we get any more humans in this compound, it's going to be a Las Vegas buffet."

Richard widened his eyes at Luke's comment, but Emily patted his hand. "He's kidding. They aren't going to eat you."

Shane narrowed his eyes. "You are under my protection, Richard."

"Perfect. You met him." Julianna shooed with her arms. "Now could everyone please get out of my room?"

Richard and Emily exchanged a look. Then

toward Shane Richard stammered out, "I want you to turn Kara back. Like you did Julianna." He waved toward the pretty blonde.

Shane gave a knowing look to Julianna and Luke. This was already starting to get out of hand and nothing much had happened yet. To Richard he answered, "I didn't turn Julianna back. She was murdered by my enemy to spite me. And your ex-wife resurrected her to use her to spy on me. It wasn't intended as a gift. She was being used."

"Oh." Richard looked truly shocked. He hadn't understood all the politics.

"He just wants things the way they were," Emily explained.

"That's the one thing I can tell you for certain is impossible." Julianna folded her arms across her chest. "Kara's life ended when she became a vampire. If she does turn back, it will be a *new* human life. I thought I explained that already?"

Richard's shoulders were slumped. He was a man used to being in control. He had run businesses and a family for years. But nothing in his life had prepared him for any of these current challenges. "It doesn't have to be like it was. I just can't stand the thought of my baby girl being a creature of the night. *Wanting* to drink blood. And enjoying the hunt."

No one said anything for a moment. They all knew that Kara was one of the fiercest hunters and potential warriors they had. They knew she enjoyed being a vampire.

Shane remembered his first few nights as a vampire and how confusing it had all been. He imagined that was where this man was now. Shane placed a hand on Richard's shoulder and the older man didn't flinch. "Richard. I know this must be a difficult time for you. But you must understand. This world exists and Kara is a part of it. And she's happy to be a part of it. You can't wish any of it away, no matter how hard you try. I've accepted witches, a vampire's mortal enemy, into my home and accepted them as family. You can too, if you give it a chance."

Richard just stared at Shane, dumbfounded. He

felt so out of his element.

"Come on, Dad." Emily tugged her father's arm. "Let's go."

Richard was heavy on his feet, and stumbled toward Julianna's bedroom door, but he said nothing. He allowed Emily to drag him from the room. He'd thought he'd had the perfect solution to all their problems, but what would a vampire understand? He was a monster too.

When the door closed behind them, Camilla had stayed with Luke, Shane and Julianna. Shane reached for her hand and she took it willingly.

"This was my concern. See how quickly this can all get out of hand? He thought this was some kind of gift I gave you." Shane spoke in calm, even tones to his sister.

Julianna pursed her lips. She could see how this could make him anxious. And he was the leader. "I understand." And she wasn't lying. She did.

"Thank you, Jules." Shane almost smiled at his sister. "Have a good rest." Shane began to walk toward the door, hand in hand with Camilla. He stopped when he reached the other side of the bed and leaned in closely to Luke, words barely above a whisper so human ears wouldn't hear. "Stay with her. She'll try to go to Damian."

Luke nodded once. He was always happy to spend a day with Julianna. The morning sun may have been barely starting to show its face, but the humans in the compound had all adopted a vampire's schedule and slept during the day.

Camilla and Shane left, closing the door with a soft click behind them. Luke kneeled on Julianna's bed and outstretched his arms. She smiled, even as she chastised herself for not being stronger around him. Even if she was a weak human, he still seemed to love and accept her. Walking on her knees on top of the bed toward him, she slapped his shoulder as hard she could. Which he barely felt.

"Was that foreplay?" Luke asked, raising an eyebrow.

"No, it's because I'm still mad at you for calling

me weak." But the twinkle in her eye belied her words. She didn't seem mad at all. She looked playful.

"Is that so, Miss Walker?" Luke smirked playfully back. "Then I shall spend my immortal life making it up to you." He embraced her and swept her onto her back, head on the pillow, so fast she barely knew what was happening. He kissed her gently. Despite being a vampire, and a consummate flirt, he had always been tender with her. Even when she was a vampire. She had always been surprised by his reverence and gentleness toward her.

So she felt no fear now, lying in the arms of a vampire. She kissed him back, grabbing the back of his head and letting her fingers slip into his perfectly placed hair.

As he continued to kiss her, holding her close to his chest, she remembered the time she had first met him escaping the cage with her brother. And the times he had protected her even when she didn't need protecting. And the little things, like opening a door for her or letting her enter a room first.

He might be a vampire, but Luke was no monster. She knew that.

"I love you, Luke." Julianna let the words slip out of her mouth breathlessly in between kisses. She hadn't meant to say it, but it was the way she felt.

Luke froze and opened his eyes to stare into hers. She suddenly worried she'd made a big mistake, acted too human. But then he caressed her blonde curls, and a smile broke out on his lips. "No one has said that to me in a really long time."

He could hear her heart pounding in her chest, a sound he hadn't heard from a lover in centuries. She looked away as she responded, "Well, it's true. I might be human and it might be complicated, but that's how I feel."

He kissed her gently. "I love you too, Julianna Walker. I loved you from the first minute I saw you. Vampire or human. It's *you* that I love." He leaned in close and just before he kissed her again, he said, "But don't tell Shane. He'll kill me."

Julianna laughed. She threw her arms around

his neck and kissed the vampire in her bed. She had known all along it was futile. Human or no, she couldn't stay mad at him. He was too important to her.

13

Despite the events of the previous night, the compound spent a restful day. The house was quiet while vampires slept and witches snoozed or quietly practiced their craft by themselves. There was an occasional soft voice floating through the halls, but it was subdued and blended into the white noise of the day. The grandfather clock from the front entryway rhythmically kept track of time, its tick-tock echoing throughout the empty halls.

Shane slept, holding Camilla tight, but he couldn't shake the feeling that this peace was somehow a foreboding. The calm gentleness of the day might be soothing to some, but it had the opposite effect on him. It foreshadowed events he had to somehow prevent, and he wasn't exactly sure how.

He would never say it out loud, but in some ways he envied Julianna. To walk away from this responsibility, to live a quiet life somewhere with Camilla and a family—it was very tempting. And this ability to sense things and know things—with no idea how he did—was a curse. He fervently wished he could lie in ignorant bliss like the other vampires, waiting for an end they never knew for sure was coming.

But Shane knew.

Pulling his arm away from Camilla, he moved to lie on his back and stare at the ceiling. It was evening now, and he knew that soon the compound would come to life. And he would need to go feed. It had been a while.

His stirring woke Camilla and she turned under the covers to face him.

"The prophecy?" Camilla asked. How she knew him so well after such a short time always rattled him.

"I was thinking...what if," Shane stated. He felt a

need to be honest. If he couldn't be honest with Camilla, who could he be honest with? And he didn't want to keep it inside.

"What if?" Camilla propped up on an elbow, her brown hair cascading down her shoulder. "Meaning, Julianna may have a point?"

Shane turned his gaze to Camilla. For a moment he just watched her, studying the perfect lines of her face. "I have to stop the curse, right?"

Camilla placed a hand on top of his bare chest. "You keep calling it a curse. Maybe it's just a prophecy. And maybe you spend too much time and energy worrying about it."

Shane stared back up at the ceiling. For sure he was spending too much time focused on the prophecy. It had consumed his entire immortal existence. "It's a curse to take immortality away from them without it being their choice. And I'm their leader. I have to protect them."

Camilla nuzzled back down and rested her head on his shoulder. She longed to take away some of his burden in whatever way she could. His sense of duty had always been one of the things she loved about him. "Is it possible that you don't have to take sides? I mean, Julianna and Damian have a point of view, and Kara and Isabelle have a point of view. Could it be that both are right in their own ways?"

Shane didn't answer. If it wasn't a fact he could foresee, he would likely agree with Camilla. Why would he mind if Damian wanted to be human again? He could respect that. But the fact that it triggered so much more is what made him pause. "If I can stop Julianna and Damian, I can stop the curse."

"What are you going to do?"

"Still working out the details. But when the time comes, will you help me?"

"You know I will." Camilla leaned in to kiss him and the door swung wide open, hitting the wall hard.

"Let's go hunting," Isabelle shouted, completely ignoring the intimate moment she had walked in on. "Luke's on babysitting duty and Kara just went last night."

Shane stood, dressing himself in black jeans and a black T-shirt. "Yeah. I need to."

Camilla sat up in bed, the covers falling to her lap. "Shane. It's gonna be okay." She was finishing the previous conversation, but Isabelle assumed she was talking about hunting.

"Yeah, we're vampires. It's what we do. Don't be clingy."

But Shane understood and he sat back down on the bed next to Camilla, placing a hand behind her neck. "I know. We're going to find a way." He kissed her good-bye and she fought the urge to grab him and keep him with her. But she knew he needed to feed. And running, preying and killing would be good for him. She didn't dare judge. She had killed people, too.

"Let's go into the city this time," Isabelle smiled with wicked glee. She was looking forward to the night out with Shane. They could've run at vampire speed and perhaps gone unnoticed, but half the fun was blending in. So Isabelle led him to the garage where they each grabbed a motorcycle and drove toward their destination.

Hunting at dusk was not as easy as it was at midnight. But, of course, for Isabelle, easy was boring. She preferred the challenge of outwitting and luring her prey with light still creeping across the sky, versus lying in wait under the cover of darkness.

And for Shane, hunting was a means to an end. He needed to feast on human blood to survive. Finding a victim in the morning, evening, middle of the night...it usually made no difference to him.

But today was different.

Today he wanted to vent his frustrations. To take the weight off his shoulders and funnel it into the act of killing. Today he felt like a vampire.

Isabelle had led them to a restaurant packed with people. Tables were filled, and still-hungry patrons packed the lobby and even more waited right outside the storefront. There was pop music reverberating from the speakers to set the mood. Isabelle found it annoying, but she pushed past it because of the buffet of feasting options this place always presented.

Stubby's Bar and Grill on Sepulveda always packed in the patrons.

"Follow me," Isabelle beckoned to Shane. She walked slowly through the gathered crowd in front of the restaurant, seductively shaking her hips and flirting with the men. Shane fought the urge to grab the first guy he saw and rip him limb from limb. He had always wanted to be more than a monster, but tonight he didn't feel like fighting it.

He followed Isabelle into the restaurant and then turned left, just as she did, ducking into a bar. The lights were dimmed, barely lighting the room a touch more than the natural evening glow already had. And just like the rest of the restaurant, the room was packed. Every seat at the bar was taken and tables were filled. Many patrons just decided to stand with their drink in hand, talking to their buddies.

"May I have this seat?" Isabelle spoke coyly to a middle-aged gentleman at the end of the bar. He was dressed professionally, and Shane assumed he was drinking away his guilt from swindling old ladies out of their insurance money all day. At any rate, he doubted his contribution to humanity was all that significant.

The man scrambled off his chair with a dumb look on his face. Shane knew Isabelle had compelled him, although she didn't really need to. He would've given her his seat just because she was beautiful.

She turned to the man seated on her other side. "And my friend would like your seat, please." A little more drunk, he reacted more slowly, but also eventually relinquished his chair for Shane.

Shane sat in the bar stool Isabelle had procured for him and asked, "So what's your game?"

Isabelle shrugged and then glanced around the room. "Now you just pick your vic and have your fun."

"The room is mostly men. Did you just want to flirt?"

Isabelle smiled. "What? I can't help it if it's one of the tools on my belt."

Shane just shook his head. They both needed to have fun in their own way. And Isabelle was so often all business, he enjoyed seeing this side of her.

Shane leaned into Isabelle and then pointed to a man seated at a high-top table just a few feet from them. He was leaning back in his chair, long hair slicked back. He was dressed fashionably and had the look of someone who knew how handsome he was. "How about that guy?"

He looked like he might be on a double date. He was there with another man and two women. Isabelle nodded. "A solid contender." She then pointed to the man working hastily behind the bar. "I've been trying to get that guy for months."

Shane saw a young, clean-cut man focused intently on making drinks for his customers. He had a look about him of maybe someone ex-military. He instantly understood Isabelle's attraction. "The bartender?"

She nodded. "His name is Jack. How cute is that?"

Shane raised an eyebrow. "I don't see you with cute."

"I'm not going to marry the guy. Once I bite him, I can't come back here, anyway."

A very drunk man stumbled up behind Shane and tapped him on the shoulder. He looked about thirty, with five-o-clock stubble, and reeked of alcohol. Shane said nothing but raised an eyebrow questioningly at the guy.

"My buddies think you're a vampire. Are you a vampire?" The man slurred his words and wobbled unsteadily on his legs.

Isabelle laughed and the whole thing amused Shane. So he asked, "What makes you guys think that?"

With a floppy hand, the man gestured at Shane and his all-black outfit. "Look at you. You *look* like every vampire movie ever made."

Shane looked at Isabelle, who was trying to hide her laughter behind her hand. "I like this guy," she said.

Shane turned back to the drunk man. He likely wouldn't remember much of this the next day, and anyway everyone would blame the alcohol. So he decided to have some fun with the man. "Not only am I a vampire, I am *the* vampire." And he finished the sentence with elongated fangs an inch from the man's face. He added a hiss for additional effect.

The drunk man stumbled backward, tripping on a table and spilling the drinks of the customers sitting there. Ignoring the destruction, keeping his eyes on Shane, he ran from the bar as fast as his drunk, wobbly legs could take him.

Shane and Isabelle enjoyed the good laugh.

"Can I buy you a drink?" The handsome guy Shane had pointed out earlier had waltzed up to Isabelle and spoken breathily into her ear.

To Shane she said, "Normally, this would be far too easy, but today I'll take the win."

Shane gestured to the guy. "I'm sure you can still toy with him and have some fun."

Isabelle turned back to the handsome guy. "I'm Isabelle."

He leaned into the counter, completely oozing with cockiness. Shane had to suppress his laughter at this guy. So full of himself he had no idea what web he was about to walk into. "Xavier."

In a silky voice Shane had never heard her use, Isabelle said "Come with me." And she grabbed Xavier's hand and marched toward the restrooms. With a dopey half-smile, the cocky guy followed the beautiful seductress. Whatever he imagined was about to happen, Shane was certain he was unprepared for the reality.

"You're in my seat," a scruffy voice echoed in Shane's ear. Without turning around, Shane indicated Isabelle's now vacant seat. The scruffy man leaned in closer with his stale breath filling Shane's nostrils and said, "I don't think you heard me. I want *this* seat."

Ah, so he wanted to pick a fight and thought Shane would be an easy win. It was easy to think that. Shane looked young and fit, but not especially tough or strong. He turned around to stare and the stinky-breathed man. He was a bit taller than Shane and thick, but not in the way of someone who pumped iron. He was broad-shouldered and looked like a man who once might have dreamed of a football career and now simply ate and drank his feelings.

And Shane saw in his mind's eye that this man loved cruelty. In fact, Shane knew he had recently shot a man dead and had thus far gotten away with it. He would make a perfect vampire's victim. Rid the world of his kind of evil. But Shane didn't want to make a scene here in the restaurant.

So, worldlessly, Shane pushed the air in front of the man and he slid back uncontrollably toward the entryway to the bar. The man had a look of confusion, maybe even a little fear, as he slid having no clue what had caused it.

Slowly, Shane stood up and followed the man to the lobby of the restaurant. The man was gathering his bearings and was not quite as full of piss and vinegar as he had been a moment ago.

When he made it to the confused man, Shane said, "Let's continue this lovely conversation outside, shall we?"

And without letting the man respond, Shane

gripped his elbow so tight he couldn't have wiggled out if he'd wanted to. He forcibly led the man outside where the evening dusk was now disappearing and the nighttime sky was beginning to take over.

The crowds of people moved aside to let them through, but if they suspected anything was off about these two, it didn't faze them. They kept talking and laughing, waiting for their opportunity to dine inside.

And Shane kept dragging the stinky-breathed man by his elbow until they were around the side of the building. A streetlight lit up the small alleyway that sat between the restaurants, but otherwise it was dark. Trash littered the ground all around a dumpster, as if the act of putting it inside the trash can were just too daunting. Near the dumpster, Shane pushed stinky-man up against the wall.

"So, you like hurting people, huh?" Shane asked, and then stood there casually, picking a nail.

The man was confused at being slid across the room and dragged by a young man half his age and size, but something in him made him want to show bravado. He never in a million years expected this blonde kid to be a threat. And if shit were going down, he was going to go down swinging.

Stinky-man spit a giant wad of phlegm onto Shane's shoes. "You wanna fight? Let's fight." And he got in a power stance, fists up in front of his face. He looked like a man who might actually know what he was doing in a boxing ring.

But that's not where any of this was headed. As if the man were boring him, Shane dropped his arms and sighed. And then let his fangs extend, flashing a predatory grin. "I hate bullies."

It all happened in a moment.

Stinky-man, suddenly realizing that it was no ordinary man who had dragged him out of the restaurant and behind a dumpster, began to panic. He opened his mouth to plead for the same mercy so many had begged from him in the past, only never gotten. He wouldn't get it either.

Shane knew that sometimes justice was a bitch. And he didn't want to hear the man whine, so he slid an extended claw along his throat, immediately severing the arteries, allowing the blood to spray wildly. And, most importantly, to silence Stinky-man for good.

And just as his throat began to burn with the craving, Shane latched his mouth to the open neck wound and began to drink his fill.

Isabelle's approach was a bit different.

She had led Xavier by the hand into the women's restroom, locking the door behind her. He lifted her onto the counter and she let him think he was controlling the situation. She wrapped her legs around his waist and leaned her head back, allowing him to kiss her neck. She hoped her body might distract him—she didn't want his lips anywhere near her mouth.

He slid his mouth hastily, and a bit sloppily, down to her cleavage and, as he kissed her chest, he unceremoniously grabbed her left breast. It was forceful and manic, leaving Isabelle to wonder if this guy had any clue at all how to please a woman. She couldn't help but roll her eyes, and then she moaned, pretending to like it. He yanked down the shoulders of her dress, exposing her from the waist up, curious where this was going to go. He suckled her nipple and rubbed her thigh, inching his way upward. This wasn't the worst thing he'd done to her, but Isabelle was forced to think of the litany of better lovers she'd had in her time.

So much cockiness but then no follow through.

Suddenly, Xavier stood up straight and dropped his slacks down to his ankles.

"On your knees," he instructed.

Isabelle smiled. She kinda liked how he was playing the boss with her. It was the tiniest bit of a turn-on and she wished he'd done it sooner. She stood, playing with her hair coyly, a grin still dancing across her lips. She let her tongue slide suggestively across her lower lip and then got down to groin level. Xavier leaned his head way back in anticipation.

He was nuts if he thought he was going to yank her boob and then get a blowjob. *You gotta give me something if you want something in return, she thought.* So she bit him, full fang, right in the testicles. He let out a sharp squeal, but then he slowly relaxed as the venom did its trick and she drained his blood from his body through his junk. As the blood left his body, he began to slide against the wall until he was seated before her.

Isabelle kept drinking from his groin.

Until there was a pounding at the door.

"Just a minute," Isabelle called, sitting up and wiping the trickles of blood from her chin. She yanked his pants up back to his waist, covering the bite marks, and then stood up to survey the scene. Satisfied that he looked like someone who might've just passed out, Isabelle adjusted her top back to a socially acceptable level, smoothed out her hair and then opened the door.

The woman standing there stared with her mouth wide open, looking from Isabelle to the man slumped in a heap on the floor.

"Some people just can't hold their liquor," Isabelle quipped as she shook her head and pushed past the woman still standing there in shock.

Now to find Shane. He wasn't anywhere in the bar anymore, and she was glad. That hopefully meant he was feeding. Not that Shane needed a babysitter—she could've left him—but she had never liked ditching a hunting party. She stepped out the front of the restaurant and closed her eyes to better let her hearing take over. Near her was the hum of voices, the white noise created by a collection of people talking. But just to her right, she heard the glorious sound of a vampire sucking a vein while the heartbeat slowly gets fainter.

Even as her belly was full from Xavier's blood, she found herself getting thirsty again at the sound.

She rounded the corner at a slight jog and found what she expected to see. Shane was devouring a huge man's neck, blood splattered everywhere, the neck flaps flopping under the violent force of Shane's eating.

"You still eat like a toddler, Shane." Isabelle crossed her arms and leaned on one hip. It was too early in the evening to just stroll out of there with him looking like that. Shane was covered in blood, from his blonde curls down to his black pants.

Shane looked up at Isabelle, wide-eyed, and said, "Oh, shit."

"It's fine. We'll speed walk, no one will notice," Isabelle answered.

"No, it's not that." Shane shook his head.

"Oh. Well, don't worry about the fat guy. I'm sure he was a complete douche."

Shane looked down at the large man he had annihilated. "He was. Barely even human. But it's not that either."

"Okay?" Isabelle responded in a way that was both an answer and a question.

"It's Julianna. She snuck out and she's on her way to meet with Damian."

Isabelle dropped her shoulder as the realization struck. This was the beginning of the end. "Oh, shit."

And Shane nodded.

14

"You know you didn't have to come, but I'm glad you did." Julianna spoke to Henna as they again traipsed through the mountains on their way to meet with Damian. This time to end his vampire life forever.

"You know you can't do this without me," Henna said matter-of-factly.

"I could've found another witch," Julianna responded, but she didn't really believe those words. The chances of her finding another witch willing and able before Shane could stop her were slim to none. And she knew she could never have snuck out of the compound, and Luke's watchful eye, without a witch's hex.

"Well, I believe in what you're doing." Henna

moved a branch out of the way so she could move underneath it. "No one should be forced to be something they don't want to be because of other people's fear."

Julianna found her footing on the rough terrain. Leaves and twigs crunched underneath. "So, you don't think I should feel bad if I bring about the end of vampires?"

Henna snorted. "Shame on your brother for making you feel everything is your fault. Damian wants to change. I want to help. Other vampires are inspired by Damian. This is all so much bigger than you."

Julianna was pensive for a moment, letting Henna's words soak in. Of course, Henna was right. Julianna couldn't kill and then resurrect a vampire, let alone a whole race of them, on her own. But she still felt a tingle of guilt. The kind of guilt you could bury, swallow deep down, but then, even as small as it might be, it would bubble to the surface every now and again just to remind you it was still there. "There's just something in me that tells me I'm doing the right thing. And I have to follow that."

It was now close to midnight, but there were no clouds in the sky, so the moon hung large and bright above them. Even before her vampire days, Julianna had always loved the nighttime. It was so peaceful. The noises of the world had mostly died down by now, leaving only the scurrying of nocturnal animals and the breeze rustling nature. Sure, predators came out at night. Hell, she had been one. But even that was graceful and hidden in shadows. Daylight exposed all the world's ugliness.

"I'm very grateful to your brother for accepting us witches into his compound. No other vampire in centuries has ever done that. But," Henna sighed a small sigh, "if the worst thing that comes of all of this is that there are no more vampires walking the earth preying on humans, I don't see how that's such a bad thing."

Julianna suddenly stopped and turned on Henna. "But what if there are other repercussions?

Like what if it ends witches too?"

Henna twisted her lips for a second before shrugging. "Then I'd say we've done the world some good. Not all witches are bad, just as all vampires aren't, but many of them are. Look at Theresa. If we take more Theresas out of this world...we're heroes."

"Good. I just wanted to make sure you were really committed. Because they are here and we have to hurry. I don't have much of a head start on Shane." Julianna turned back around and picked up her pace.

When they made it out of the trees and into the clearing, Notch and Damian were standing there. Damian swayed back and forth, but to Julianna he appeared much calmer than she expected. When she had been killed by Dimas, she hadn't seen or known it was coming. It was over so quickly, she had no time to think or worry. Damian is standing here knowing he dies tonight. And still he's so cool and collected.

Damian smiled when he saw the two women. "You came."

Julianna nodded. "Of course. But we need to

act fast. Not all vampires support this decision and we could be interrupted at any moment."

"Shane?" Damian asked, peering behind Julianna as if he expected him to appear.

"He's afraid this leads to the fulfillment of the Dark Prophecy," Julianna stated flatly.

"The same prophecy that he gladly fulfilled when it put him on top?" Damian asked.

Julianna frowned, sensitive as she was about that part of the prophecy. After all, *she* was the one who made sure Shane fulfilled his role. But Henna answered, "That's the very one."

Notch snickered and then said, "Maybe no one can stop it anyway. Even the powerful chosen one."

"Whether he can or he can't," Julianna responded, still frowning—she *did* believe Shane was powerful enough to stop this— "if we hurry, he can't stop us from giving Damian back his human life. We can at least do one good thing."

Damian nodded at Notch. "I'm ready." Notch pulled a blindfold out of his pocket and used it to cover

Damian's eyes. As he tied it tightly, Damian said, "Thank you, Julianna. And witch. I'm forever grateful."

Julianna slowly pulled a wooden stake out of her backpack. It was easy to come by—all the witches had them in their arsenals. Even though she knew Damian had super hearing, she didn't want him to be completely aware that she was preparing the death blow. "I'm happy to support you in this, Damian. And when you're human again, let's remain friends."

"I'd like that." Damian grinned beneath the blindfold and Julianna nodded toward Notch, who gripped Damian's arms to hold them firm behind his back. Even though Damian knew this was the first step, the urge to defend one's own life could be strong, and a small backhand would send Julianna flying across the clearing.

The second Damian's arms were behind his back, Julianna raised the stake high above her and shoved with all her might into Damian's chest. It pierced the flesh and he reacted, but it clearly hadn't penetrated his heart. So Henna helped Julianna and they shoved with all their might, leaning both their weights into the wooden stake.

Damian became dead weight in Notch's arms and his body was laid gently on the grass. Notch caressed Damian's forehead, staring at his lifeless form. Damian was dead. Step one complete.

Julianna, breathless, looked over her shoulder. "We must hurry, Henna."

"I know." Henna began pulling vials and potions out of the backpack as quickly as she could. "You'll both have to play a part if this is going to work."

Notch kept stroking Damian's hair as Henna prepared the necromancy spell. She was shaking ever so slightly as she did so. She had been a part of this spell only once—and that was to resurrect Julianna. Dealing with life-or-death spells was always a bit tricky. And she hadn't thought about the pressure until she was here under its weight. Shane was coming. Damian's life was in her hands. Julianna and Notch were counting on her. In fact, the whole Dark Prophecy now laughed in her ear mockingly.

Suddenly, Notch stood up straight. "They're coming," he announced.

Henna wiped a bead of sweat from her upper lip. "Hold hands. Now." Henna quickly lined the ingredients all around the body, just as she'd seen Theresa do with Julianna. It was sloppy and irreverent, not at all her preferred way to do magic. But the countdown clock had begun. Out of her pocket she pulled the switchblade. "Quickly. Cut your hand and let your blood drip on the ingredients of the potion."

Henna was first. She sliced and squeezed, letting the blood drip all around Damian's lifeless body. Then she handed the knife to Julianna, who stared horrified, wide-eyed and frozen at the prospect. Knowing time was running out, Henna grabbed her hand and forced the incision, then she shook Julianna's hand over the ingredients and handed the knife to Notch. "Now."

He did the same and the potion began smoking, just as it had with Julianna. Henna took it as a good sign, but she could only hope it was enough blood.

They'd had a lot more witches participating when Julianna was resurrected.

Grabbing Notch's and Julianna's hands, Henna lifted her own up to the sky.

A rustling in the trees nearby signaled time was up.

"Say the spell. Now!" Notch instructed, his fangs elongating with his panic.

Faster than she would have wanted to, Henna recited the incantation. "Gehennam ignis superextendam in artus!"

Shane, Luke, Isabelle, Kara and Elias broke through the trees.

"Again!" Notch shouted.

Trying her best to ignore the newly arrived vampires, Henna began again, "Gehennam ignis superextendam in artus!"

But she had barely gotten the words out when she went flying across the clearing.

"Shane, no!" she heard Julianna scream, as Notch protectively stood in front of Damian's still lifeless body.

Pushing off the ground, only to discover her arm was broken, Henna shoved the bone back into place and attempted to scramble back to Damian and her mini-circle of magic. While he was still ten feet from where she was crawling, Shane lifted her without the use of touch and held Henna high in the air.

"I can't let you do this," Shane announced. Julianna kept screaming in the background, both she and Notch protectively covering Damian's remains.

Henna tried to reach for Julianna, to somehow break out of Shane's powerful grip, but the effort was futile. So Henna persevered in the only way she could think of: she continued reciting the spell.

She looked up to the sky and shouted, "Gehennam ignis superextendam in artus," and hoped it was enough. Her voice was then cutoff as Shane pulled a very Theresa-like move and force-choked her from where he stood. Henna grabbed at her throat uselessly, clawing and struggling for the air she couldn't pull into her lungs.

Julianna looked down at Damian and then at her brother. She was so torn. Does she stay here and protect Damian? Or does she run to her brother and beg him to stop? Both were likely wasted efforts. All her brother had to do was send a fireball to Damian's body and it was all over.

"Let the witch go," a voice boomed and echoed as another group of vampires entered the clearing behind Damian and Notch.

Johann stood in the moonlight, his long hair untied and blowing in the wind. He didn't look menacing. He looked tired.

Shane, still holding Henna high in the air but loosening the grip on her throat a bit, stared back at his elder. "They are attempting to resurrect Damian. To turn him back into a human."

Johann let a heavy sigh escape his lips. "I know, Shane. We all do." And then he gestured behind himself and there were a number of vampires Shane had never met before, but there were also quite a few he recognized. Alexi and Regina both also stood among them.

Shane lowered Henna and then handed her to Isabelle and Elias. He didn't trust her not to run right back to Damian and finish the spell. And then, with a glare toward his uncooperative sister, he walked to Johann and his group of protesters.

"I've had a vision," Shane explained. That was all they needed. An explanation. They were here protecting Damian because they thought Shane was being unreasonable. Once they heard his rationale, they would support him completely. "This very act starts the second prophecy. Our species will begin its end tonight if I don't stop this resurrection."

Shane looked at Johann's eyes. The eyes that had always held wisdom and experience. Eyes he had always trusted. But now they looked heavy and sad. There was a war going on inside Johann's mind, and Shane could see that his words hadn't sealed the result he'd wanted.

With a frown, Johann said, "I know, Shane. I know that you are trying to do the right thing. But…"

Johann looked up to the sky as if the very moon itself would provide the words he needed to have this conversation with the most powerful vampire who'd ever lived. "But we think you should just let it all play out."

"What?" Shane recoiled as if Johann had struck him, the shock from his words as powerful as a physical blow. "We have to stop the prophecy."

Johann folded his hands together in front of him reverently and bowed his head. "The Dark Prophecy began with your resurrection and it cannot be stopped."

"*I* can stop it," Shane shouted back. With a sneer he shouted, "You want to be human?"

Regina shuddered beside Johann and muttered, "Disgusting."

"This is our fate, Shane," Johann stated simply.

"Bullshit," Isabelle shouted from across the clearing.

"I hate to go against you, Shane, but we can't live with a leader who won't let us be who we want to be. Let Damian have a chance at the human life he asked for," Johann stated flatly, completely devoid of emotion. It was clear this was all weighing heavily on his heart, but he swallowed that down to stand up for Damian.

"His human life"—Shane pointed at Damian's body, his fangs elongating as he became more heated with emotion— "will cost you your immortal one. Are you willing to pay that price? I am protecting us all."

"Damian was a coward who chose a coward's way out," Isabelle shouted again from across the clearing.

Notch took exception to her words and stood with a murderous look in his eyes. Sensing that the situation was quickly getting out of control, Julianna ran to her brother, putting herself between him and the vampires that sided with her point of view.

"Shane," Julianna lowered her eyes and spoke softly. Her heart thudded in her chest but she forced herself to remain calm and keep her voice even. "Shane, listen to me. It doesn't have to end in violence.

But you need to listen to Johann. He's asking for the freedom of choice."

"This is bigger than you, Julianna. This is bigger than all of us," Shane explained to his sister. He was painfully aware of the blood still dripping from the wound on her hand, the drip, drip, as it fell on the ground. Her human scent was intoxicating and distracting. But he forced himself to focus, ignoring the siren's call that was likely distracting every immortal in the clearing.

He'd always known how stubborn she could be, so he doubted he could sway her with words. But she was human now, so he well knew he had the power here.

"You can't just leave Damian dead," Julianna begged, tears welling in her eyes. She was begging for Damian's life, but in a way she was begging for her own. She was the chance at redemption that some of them sought after. And if they were wrong, then so was she.

"You killed him," Shane shouted at his sister.

"I don't want to be human again at all," Regina stated. She looked at her nails as if they were the most important thing happening in the clearing right now. "But I don't want to live at gunpoint. I hate that shit. If I decide I want to be human, I should have that right."

"And to be honest," Alexi added, "what could you do about it if more of us chose to be human? Even you, as powerful as you are, cannot be everywhere at once. We just need a witch."

"It's time to stop fighting, Shane," Johann said again. "Let the witch finish the ceremony."

Shane looked back at Henna. She was held by Elias and Isabelle, but she didn't struggle at all. She stood there calmly, a bit defiantly, but not fighting back against her captors. She had her reasons for helping Julianna. And then he looked at Kara. Such a fierce vampire for someone so young. And her father wanted to take that away so he could selfishly have her back to himself. Where would this all end? If he gave in now and let Damian be resurrected, which vampires would have free choice and which would be victims to the prophecy?

From the day he discovered he was the chosen one, the burden had been heavy on his conscience. He was just a kid himself. A young man who liked to surf and play music, hanging out with friends. He hadn't a care in the world. And he'd never asked for any of this. But it had come to him. No matter what path he'd chosen, it would've found him. It had always been looking for him.

But now the choice was his.

And he chose the role he was resurrected to play. He was the leader of the vampires and he felt the responsibility of that. He knew that meant saving them all, even if it was saving them from themselves.

He looked back at Johann and Regina and their posse. They'd surprised him. He knew they didn't want to be human. Why could they not respect his decision? How could he make them see reason? Shane *knew* this was the beginning of the end. And he couldn't just stand by and watch.

"No." Shane spoke in a low voice. "I have to

protect us all. It's my duty. Now please leave so I can stop the prophecy."

Johann looked back at the vampires gathered around him. Regina pursed her lips but said nothing. Johann shook his head as he turned back to Shane. "So be it."

And with a heavy heart, Johann ran at vampire speed toward Shane's middle, taking him by surprise before he could use his power against them. The vampires that had come with Johann ran toward Isabelle, Kara, Elias and Luke.

And Damian's body lay lifeless there in the clearing, as each side fought for their very survival.

15

Johann had hoped to take Shane by surprise, but that was easier said than done and he hadn't been successful in his attempt. Shane reacted quickly, stopping Johann in his tracks with a powerful force of air that sent Johann skidding backward.

Meanwhile, seeing the vampires coming toward them at breakneck speed, Isabelle and Elias shoved Henna out of the way and she landed on the ground near Julianna and Damian. Notch stood over them, choosing to protect Damian and the humans like an immortal bodyguard. They all watched as Regina flew at Luke and Alexi jumped toward Elias.

Claws and fangs ripped and tore at flesh and clothing.

Kara was fast, climbing on the back of the female vampire who had chosen her, likely seeing Kara as an easy target. But Kara wasn't as fragile as she appeared, and she demonstrated that when she bit into the vampire's neck, pulling away with a mouthful of blood. The woman she fought didn't give up either, and she rolled on the ground to get Kara off. It worked, and from the ground, the woman slashed her claws across Kara's chest, ripping her shirt and leaving giant claw marks in Kara's chest.

But Kara was a natural reborn vampire, and this only served to inspire her, just as it would have done to Isabelle. Kara hissed and then ran at her attacker again, biting the first thing she could reach— her arm.

Isabelle was fighting a young man she thought was handsome. Regardless of whether or not they were there to stop the prophecy or let vampires have the right to choose, the politics meant nothing to Isabelle. She was here for Shane. And she was itching for a fight anyway. Like her victim at Stubby's earlier in the night, this handsome guy was sloppy. He came at her with floppy arms and legs, so with barely an effort, Isabelle lifted her leg and straightened it right in his chest. He slid backward and landed on his knees. This might get boring. She could fight this guy off and get her nails done at this rate.

Despite her own back and forth with the female vampire, Kara saw Isabelle's kick and reached out to give her a high-five. At Kara's distraction, the female tried to lunge for Kara's neck, but Isabelle saw her and lifted her by her throat, tossing her far away from Kara.

Kara smiled through bloody teeth, "You're such a badass."

Behind them, Regina tore at Luke. Neither one of them was the best fighter in the vampire clan. But they had history, and a small piece of each of them was enjoying the back and forth. Regina, for years of being rejected by Luke after one unforgettable night. They could have been great together, a glorious power couple. And Luke, for years of being punished by Regina because he didn't want to be her boy toy.

With a swipe of her extended claws, Regina ripped Luke's shirt clean in half, exposing his muscled torso but not damaging any flesh. He shoved her backward and she slid a few feet and then advanced again. This time she got uncomfortably close, as if she might kiss him and Luke froze in confusion. But it only lasted a second before she opened her mouth wide and sunk her fangs deep into Luke's shoulder. Luke howled in pain and he yanked her off him by pulling on her arms. She smiled wickedly as she licked his blood clean from her lips.

"What is wrong with you?" Luke asked simply, but Regina just kept smiling.

Elias, ever the soldier, was focused more on the art of war.

There wasn't a single scratch or mark on his body as he dodged, rolled, feinted and then struck, slicing his attacker with sharp claws. He was fierce, his face battle-hardened and stoic as he defended, then attacked over and over. Isabelle watched him with admiration as she hurled her assailant across the clearing. He was a beautiful specimen and even sexier when he was ripping at another vampire's flesh.

But amongst all the cacophony of vampires fighting, biting and flying through the air, Henna and Julianna sat holding vigil over Damian's remains. Julianna spared a glance at Luke, worried for his safety, but a glance was all she could give. Her attention was tightly focused on the promise she'd made Damian. And deep down she knew Luke would be fine. He had a better chance of being taken home by Regina than seriously injured.

Henna had tried a few more times to say the incantation, and still Damian lay limp on the grass. The bit of dew beginning to form on the grass was now causing all the ingredients to clump around him. Julianna had hope etched across her face. How she desperately wanted someone to be like her. To not be the only human-turned-vampire-turned-human again.

But Henna was worried they'd had to rush too much. And they hadn't had enough witches. And magic needed precision and meticulousness, neither of which they'd had the luxury of having here in the clearing under duress.

And even as Henna sat there thinking of all that had gone wrong, Damian's left foot twitched.

"Julianna, look!" Henna shouted, barely able to restrain herself. The last thing she needed was for every vampire to wonder what was happening. She pointed at his foot and Julianna smiled in return, the relief reflected in her eyes.

Then his leg kicked out and Notch turned around to watch Damian resurrect. The spell was working. Damian was slowly coming back to life.

Johann knew fighting Shane was an exercise in futility, and besides he didn't really want to hurt him. He didn't want anyone getting hurt. But he did want to buy the witch enough time to finish the spell. So he continued his feeble attempts to get at Shane. He ran right, Shane sent him flying. He came down low, Shane sent him flying. Johann tried to trick him by starting out to the right and then going left and rolling toward Shane. Shane sent him flying.

Julianna and Henna were clearly excited about something, so Johann knew he just needed another minute. He extended his fangs and claws and jumped at Shane, knowing as he did that he would never meet his foe. An invisible force shoved him high in the air and he spun like a vortex before he smashed to the ground.

But Shane had also noticed what was happening with Damian, and Johann could only hope they'd given Henna enough time.

"Enough!" Shane's thundering voice echoed through the clearing and beyond. As he shouted, he shot flames from his hands, separating vampires from one another throughout the clearing. Vampires were bloodied and haggard, but no one was truly injured. They backed away from one another, confused and slightly frightened of the fire.

Shane stole a glance over his shoulder, peering into the darkness. Silently he called to Camilla, hoping she could feel his plea. He needed her now. *It's time, Camilla.*

"It's over. The resurrection is complete," Shane announced to all the vampires in the clearing. The fighting vampires stood frozen, fear and wonder written across their faces. "The Dark Prophecy is coming true. Again."

Slowly, one by one, they all gathered around Julianna, Henna and Notch as they sat with the slowly awakening Damian. None of them had ever witnessed anything so extraordinary. Of course, they all knew Julianna's story, but thirdhand only. None of the vampires present thought they'd ever see a vampire transform to a human with their own eyes.

And then Damian sucked in a gasp of air. And opened his eyes. Human eyes.

It was Damian, and yet he was different. Isabelle, knowing him as well as she did, sensed the difference right away. He'd always been a soft vampire in her estimation, but compared to this he'd been a rock. The man before them was gentle and pliable, like a ragdoll.

"Holy shit," Isabelle breathed, covering her

mouth in shock at the sight before her.

Damian looked at all the faces surrounding him in the moonlight. He blinked twice, confusion and fear etched across his face. "Where am I?" he managed to croak.

Julianna opened her arms wide to keep the vampires at a distance from her newly awakened friend. Of course, if they wanted to get to Damian there was nothing she could really do, but it was her instinct to protect him. "When you first wake up, your brain is in a fog, like it's filled with cotton. It took me days to get all my memories back."

Johann took in a giant scent of the air all around them. He could smell Damian's blood flowing through his veins. He could hear his heart as it beat in his chest. Even the sheen of sweat forming on Damian's upper lip smelled different. In complete wonderment, Johann stated, "It worked. He's human. I can smell it."

"So, what does this mean, Shane?" Luke asked. This felt bigger than Julianna's transformation. This was the moment he'd been dreading. The beginning of the end. And he'd borne witness to it. To the event that would cause their complete annihilation as a species.

"What do you think it means?" Regina snorted sarcastically. "Maybe when you resurrect as a human, you'll actually have a bit more brains to go with that brawn."

"It means that Julianna was right all along. The Dark Prophecy cannot be stopped," Shane explained. Julianna grabbed his hand and squeezed and then looked at Luke with a small, shy smile. Neither of these men, who meant so much to her, might ever be able to forgive her, and that fractured her heart. But she knew Damian had the right to be human if he could be, and she couldn't stop fighting for that.

Johann surprised everyone by removing his coat, a long stylish one like you'd see a professional wearing on the streets of Manhattan. He dropped it in the grass where he stood and announced, "I'm next."

Regina took a giant step backward, like the

desire to be human was contagious. And, in fact, Shane knew that desire or no, humanism would spread like a disease. She shook her head vehemently. "We were just fighting for Damian's right to choose. Not to become humans ourselves."

Johann spoke so calmly, like a grandparent soothing a small child. He kept his emotions in check, even if they were just under the surface ready to burst. "I believe in the Dark Prophecy. Always have. And so I believe that the end has come. And I'm tired. Tired of the Shadow Wars and all the fighting. Tired of avoiding the sun and living in shadows for centuries. Tired of never growing old and dying a natural death. I'm ready. I'm ready to be human again, to live out my final days as a mortal man." He placed a gentle hand on Regina's arm, and she didn't pull away. "You should have the right to choose for yourself, and whatever you choose, I respect it. But I believe our kind was born of a curse, as the legend says. And if I have a chance to not be cursed anymore, I'm going to take it."

Julianna surprised Johann and everyone in the

circle by jumping up and draping her arms around his neck. It took Johann a moment to register her reaction, but then he patted her back gently. He locked eyes with Shane, who nodded in response. Damian was the trigger event he had wanted to stop, but now that his transformation was complete, Camilla was his only hope. If the back-up plan fell through, all the vampires in this circle would soon be living their final days as immortals.

Johann pulled back from Julianna with his hands on her forearms. "Julianna, would you do me the honors?"

But before Julianna could speak, Notch stood from where he'd been dutifully at Damian's side and stated, "She can't. She's too human. I'll kill you. And then someone needs to promise to kill me."

Henna helped a dazed Damian to his feet and then stated, "Wait a minute, everyone. I love the enthusiasm to un-monster yourselves, but I'm just one witch. I can't perform a mass resurrection spell by myself." With one arm around Damian's waist, she supported his weight.

Damian glanced nervous human eyes all around the circle. And it was as if he could sense the evil surrounding him. He locked eyes with Notch, but then reached for Julianna. Somehow, without his memories intact, he knew that she and Henna were the only two like him.

"Then no one kill anyone until Camilla gets here. She's on her way," Shane stated. And then he telepathically called to her again. *It's time, Camilla. I need you.*

"Why is everyone talking of killing?" Damian spoke with wide eyes to Julianna, who draped an arm around him and consoled him.

"Don't worry. It's all good. They want their monster sides to die so they can be normal humans again, like you and me."

Damian's face still reflected confusion, so if the words were connecting in his brain, it wasn't completely registering in his expressions yet. But he fell silent, watching all the monsters around him.

Afraid and confused.

"But this will spread the disease, right?" Isabelle asked. "Isn't that what you saw, Shane? If we don't want to be human, we should leave?"

"Anyone who wants to leave is free to do so. My vision did show us all transforming, whether we liked it or not. I'm not sure that I can stop that. But I still have hope that we can control the Prophecy. If you have faith in me, I ask you to stay." Shane dropped the pretense he often used like a mask to appear more like the chosen one than he felt. As he asked his friends to stay, he looked like a blonde young man, barely more than a kid. It wasn't the most powerful vampire to ever live that stood before them, it was a surfer who loved the ocean and spending time with friends. It was a kid with band posters in his childhood room. He wasn't telling them to stay as their leader, he was encouraging them to stay as their friend.

Luke folded his arms. "I'm not leaving." He had been like a brother to Shane from the start and was determined to be so to the end.

"I'll stay," Elias also announced. If fierce looks could stop the prophecy, he'd have done it a thousand times over.

Kara looked at Isabelle, planning to take her cue from her idol. Isabelle shrugged. "I've never been one for the easy way out." And then she stuck a clawed finger in Shane's face. "But if I turn human, I'm hunting you down and staking you."

Shane huffed a laugh, mostly because he believed it. Vampire or no, Isabelle was likely a force to be reckoned with.

"Shane, I'm ready," Johann said again.

"Okay. I just..." Shane looked over his shoulder for any sign of the pretty witch. There was none. He turned back to Johann and placed a gentle hand on his shoulder. "Could you just give me five minutes?"

Johann tightened his lips into a straight line. "What exactly are you cooking up?"

"I don't know if I like any of this," Regina stated with a frown.

"I wanted to try to stop Damian's

transformation—sorry, Damian," Shane explained, glancing at the confused now-human. "I wasn't trying to stop his freedom, I wanted to protect ours. But I was too late for that, and Julianna and Henna were too determined." He spared a glance at the two young women. "So now, all we can do is try to stop the unwanted spread, so no one is forced against their will to become human." He looked directly at Johann. "I *want* this to be a choice you make, and not an eradication that sweeps through us uncontrollably."

Johann nodded in understanding. He respected this plan and knew that he felt likewise. No one here, vampire, human or witch, wanted anyone to transform against their wishes.

Regina placed her hands on her hips and leaned into a pouty pose. "So again you are trusting our fate to witches?"

"No, I don't see it that way." Shane turned around to face Regina. In typical Regina fashion, she wore a top that was cut so low it left little to the imagination. Why any vampire would think that cleavage was battle armor was beyond Shane. But the look was very Regina. "I see it as friends and family helping one another, no matter what."

Regina snorted in response but said nothing further. Shane continued looking around expectantly. The only sound breaking the awkward silence was Julianna murmuring words of comfort to Damian. She understood how all of this must appear to him, waking up in the middle of fighting and debating between powerful vampires. And his own memories of being a vampire were still muddy in his brain.

And then there was a glimmer in the moonlight. The air seemed to shimmer and twist, as if it were being folded and tucked. And then Camilla appeared. But she wasn't alone. Behind her stood many of the old Harbor Coven witches, each holding a small bottle of liquid.

"I think I did it, Shane." Camilla smiled and the beauty of it washed over his sense of relief, making his throat tighten with emotion. He fought the urge to grab her and kiss her right there in the clearing.

Instead, he smiled back. "I knew you would."

Camilla began walking forward and the gathering of witches, Emily in the forefront, followed her. As they neared the vampires, Camilla held up her vial. "Everyone needs to drink this."

Isabelle hissed and stepped backward. "Like hell."

Camilla continued, ignoring Isabelle's reaction and the looks of distrust on many a vampire's face. As a witch in Theresa's coven, she had learned the art of keeping an even keel despite the goings-on around her. Camilla's head was high, her brown hair resting gently on her shoulder. "I've invented a potion that will protect you. All of you."

"But what about those of us who want to be human again like Julianna and Damian?" Johann asked.

"If you drink this,"—Camilla turned smiling eyes on Johann. She'd always had great respect for the elder— "whichever decision you make, staying a vampire or turning human, will come true once you've been killed. You'll either resurrect as a human or as a vampire, but it will be your choice."

"That's ridiculous." Regina lifted her shoulder haughtily.

"How can you possibly be sure this works? There's no way you've tested it," Isabelle stated.

"It works. I know magic," Camilla responded, as if that were all they should need to know before putting their very existence into her hands.

"I'll test it." Shane locked eyes with Camilla. Her beautiful brown eyes. He trusted her completely. He would never have any doubt about putting his life in her hands.

But others didn't necessarily see it the same way. They remembered Theresa's pretty poisonous flower, and the sliver of doubt always slipped through into their consciousness.

"No." It was Elias, literally stepping in front of Shane to physically block him from the potion. "I'll be first to test it."

"Everyone stop." Johann shoved Shane and Elias out of the way to get to Camilla. "I am the oldest vampire here *and* I want to be human. It makes the most sense for me to be the first."

Camilla raised the potion in front of him with absolute confidence radiating from her being.

"Johann..." Regina started, but Johan quickly cut her off.

"Regina, I know what I'm doing." His voice was sharp and his tone resolute.

"Camilla is one of us," Shane announced, looking at Regina but telling the whole group. "We can trust her."

Johann took the potion from Camilla and downed the brownish-green liquid in one gulp. It was hot and it burned his throat, but that helped block the nasty taste of rotten vegetables. Johann opened his mouth a few times to air out the potion flavor. And then turned to Notch. "Kill me. It's time."

"Is that it?" Isabelle asked Camilla. "Does he need to let it incubate or anything? Or he can just jump right in like that?"

Very calmly, Camilla answered Isabelle but by

talking to Johann. "Are you ready?"

Johann nodded. "I am."

"Then you're right. It's time." She looked at Notch and gave him the go ahead with a nod of her chin and a look in her eye.

In a flash, Johann was dead. Notch extended his claws and swiped fiercely at Johann's neck, severing it to the spine. It barely remained connected to his torso.

Julianna winced and shielded Damian from the blood spatter, but he did still cry out. The vampires, however, were silent. Blood and death didn't faze them and they were completely entranced in watching the potion have its affects—or not. Some witches covered their eyes from the gruesome sight, but most also watched on in curiosity. They believed in Camilla's abilities as a witch, but this surpassed magic even Theresa had ever dreamed of.

"What happens now?" Isabelle voiced what they were all thinking as they watched a nearly decapitated Johann lie lifeless on the grass.

"Now, we wait," Shane answered, and he grabbed Camilla's hand in his own, pulling her toward himself with a slight tug. She moved to stand as close to him as she could. Whatever happened next, prophecy or not, he had no intention of leaving Camilla's side. They had twisted their fates together, and he would see that through to the end.

"Don't we have to do the spell to resurrect him?" Henna asked.

From Shane's side Camilla shook her head. "The spell is roped into the potion. He will resurrect as either a human or a vampire—depending on his own heart and its desires."

As they stood there watching and waiting in the darkness of the night, it felt like days had passed instead of minutes. The silence among them dragged on, with the serenade of nocturnal critters providing the only soundtrack. Crickets chirped; mice scurried. Leaves rustled in an on-again-off-again breeze. And still they waited for Johann to emerge from death in his chosen final form.

"How long do we wait?" Luke asked. The silence and the standing around were itching at his core and making him fidgety. Despite centuries of immortality, patience still wasn't his area of strength.

"As long as it takes," Shane answered cryptically. The truth was, nobody knew. If he was being honest with himself, no one even knew that the spell would work at all. Notch might have killed Johann completely. But Shane swallowed the tiny seed of doubt, because he wanted to believe this was possible. And he believed in Camilla.

Blood had pooled all around Johann's body, forming a pond of red in the middle of the grass. Julianna and Damian still looked away, although Julianna listened intently for the sound of life returning. She wanted this to work. She wanted there to be a solution. Not just for Johann, but for her own sake, as well.

Being the person who fulfilled the Dark Prophecy twice—once with Shane and once with resurrecting Damian—wasn't something she'd asked for. But she'd help Damian again in an instant if she had the opportunity to do this night over again. Holding his warm hand and looking into his human eyes, she knew she'd done the right thing. But the guilt that followed in knowing she might've caused the eradication of their entire species—that was a lot to process. If Camilla's spell worked, she would've freed more than just the vampires tonight.

And then they heard the sound. Johann's neck twitched as the severed flesh from his wound began to stitch itself back together.

"Well, fuck me," Regina stated as she watched his wound heal itself and jerky movements begin happening to his various body parts.

"Everyone here already has, Regina," Luke announced, rolling his eyes as he made fun of her. She slapped his arm playfully, but she didn't deny anything or even have the look of someone offended.

"Moment of truth. Time to see if he is human or vampire." Letting go of Camilla's hand, Shane knelt down to be closer to his friend and councilor.

Camilla stayed standing, a look of complete confidence still defining her facial expression. She wasn't sure when she'd become a better witch than Theresa, but she'd always known she'd had the natural proclivity for it. Magic, spells and incantation were as natural to her as playing an instrument was to a fine musician. If this was all it took to relieve the burden she knew Shane was carrying, then so be it.

She didn't care in the slightest if vampires were eradicated from the earth. The Dark Prophecy meant nothing to her. But she did care about Shane. And Isabelle and Luke and Elias. They had become like family. They'd begun to fill a void that had been empty since she'd left her own parents years ago in North Carolina. And if her new family wanted to remain vampires, then she wanted to support them. She had the power to give them the choice and it felt wrong to keep that power to herself.

And it felt wrong to stand by and watch Shane anguish in knowing he couldn't help his fellow vampires. The most powerful vampire to ever live, yet he couldn't stop the prophecy. He couldn't stop some vampires from wanting to be human again. So all they could do was embrace the choice. And Camilla had fulfilled that dream.

With a supreme look of satisfaction, she watched Johann open his eyes. And heard the gasps from the vampires and witches all around her. His transformation was complete.

16

"That's it. I'm next," Notch announced, removing his jacket and gold chain so they didn't get blood on them. He loved being a vampire and living the nightlife, but he loved Damian more. He couldn't imagine an immortal life without him.

"I'm after Notch," another vampire who had come with Johann announced.

Shane stood, helping a wobbly Johann to his feet. "How much do you remember, Johann?"

Johann shook his head. "Not much. Could someone please explain to me why I am here?" Luckily, he didn't look down. He really would have questioned the pool of blood at his feet and the red liquid that dripped down his clothing.

"You were a vampire, but now you're a human again," Shane explained and then motioned to his sister. "Julianna, can you help Johann?"

Julianna looked at Damian but then saw Henna who had never left his side since his transformation. She knew between Henna and Notch he would be okay.

Johann seemed to relax when he saw her, Julianna's face triggering a memory of happy days. Details of those days were murky, but he knew she'd been a part of happy memories—that much he could piece together. She grabbed his hands and explained in soft whispers what he was going through, using her own experience and now Damian's as her playbook.

"You must drink the potion tonight," Camilla explained to the others. "Everyone must. It's the only way to be sure the choice is yours."

"And then you kill us all?" Isabelle asked skeptically.

"And what if we refuse?" Regina added.

"Listen up," Shane announced, voice echoing in the clearing. "We all must do our part to stop the human disease from taking away our will. Pair up with one of the Harbor Coven witches, drink the potion and the witch will kill you. You'll resurrect in whatever form you choose—human or vampire."

"I'm not sure I like this," Kara muttered to Isabelle.

"I never thought I'd see the day I'd willingly let a witch kill me," Isabelle replied. She turned to the nearest witch and announced, "You'd better not enjoy this."

Notch chose his witch quickly. He was ready to go. His choice had been made. Others followed suit, some with sluggish feet and others with the confidence that Notch exuded.

Shane, naturally, turned to Camilla. "Do you have another potion for me?"

"Of course, I do. And yours is different than the others." Camilla smiled as she pulled out a vial of bubbling green liquid. Where the other potions were more brown and dirty looking, Shane's was a vibrant green.

Shane raised an eyebrow.

"The choice is yours, Shane. This doesn't change that. I support you whatever form you want to take. You know that. Do you trust me?" She outstretched her hand and put the vial right in front of him.

He looked at the potion and then looked at Camilla. The hesitation had nothing to do with trust. It had to do with the choice. For everything he wanted, and everything he was, what did he truly desire to be? What choice would his heart make? As a vampire he was strong and powerful. Others looked up to him. He'd never had that as a human. If he'd stayed human, he'd likely still be working a minimum wage job and hanging out with buddies smoking weed. What would he be going back to? And yet, what life would he have with Camilla—what could he offer her—as a vampire? Powerful or no, he was still a bloodthirsty creature of the night.

Feeling pulled in two directions, he decided not to overthink it. He grabbed the potion and swallowed it down quickly. It coated his tongue like medicine, leaving a bitter aftertaste that made him want to gag. When he looked up from the potion, he saw Camilla standing there in the moonlight with a wooden stake in her hands, a single tear rolling down her cheek. The gravity of what she had to do was getting to her emotions.

"Be strong, Camilla," Shane encouraged her. "I'll come back in no time."

"What if you don't remember me when you resurrect?" Camilla asked with a catch in her throat.

Shane saw a loose tendril of brown hair and he tucked it gently behind her ear. And then he stepped close to her, so close they were breathing the same air, and he kissed her tenderly on the lips. "How could I ever forget you?" He stepped back and squeezed her hands one last time before saying, "You can do this, Camilla. I've made my choice."

"I love you," Camilla told him. And then she raised her arm and delivered the final death blow.

As Camilla sobbed over Shane's lifeless body

lying there in the grass, shaking with the emotions of what she'd had to do, Kara turned with wild, fearful eyes to her sister, Emily.

"If I run, what then?" Kara asked with a tremor in her voice.

Calmly, evenly, as only a big sister can, Emily explained, "Then you risk becoming a human whether you like it or not and causing others to become human against their will." Emily stepped forward, the bottle of potion firmly in her grasp. "Don't worry. If you are confident in your choice, then this will be easy."

"I am," Kara said with her chin outstretched. She didn't appear as confident as she was trying to convince her sister she was.

"Kara, you know I don't care if you're a vampire. You are always going to be my sister, no matter what. Choose what you want." Emily held the vial up to Kara, and after a moment's hesitation, Kara took the vial and drank it quickly, gagging as all the others had done.

Emily pulled out her stake.

Kara locked eyes with her sister. "I'd better resurrect."

"You will. And then you can finally live a life with no Dark Prophecy hanging over you." And Emily stabbed her sister swiftly in the heart, and then held her in her arms as she crumpled to the ground. Emily trembled from emotion, but she didn't cry. She knew her sister would awaken in the form she chose, and that was all she could want for Kara: for Kara to be who she'd always wanted to be.

Emily sat in the clearing smoothing her sister's forehead and waiting for her resurrection. All around her, vampires were drinking the potion and dying at a witch's hand. Emily watched Julianna as she took in the scene that she had caused. Her face was stoic, but Emily noticed that she was watching very carefully, as if the vampire's choices were somehow a part of her. Johann, at her side, watched in complete horror.

Notch was the first to awaken. Not surprisingly, he was human. His witch helped him to his feet and explained to him what was going on. And slowly others began to show signs of life. A twitch here. A shake there. Gasping for air or convulsing back to life.

Camilla knelt at Shane's side, holding his hand. It seemed like he was taking forever. Everyone was reawakening around him, and yet he remained still, lying on the grass, lips blue and body pale. Julianna left Johann and ran to her brother's other side, kneeling in the grass across from Camilla. "Come on, Shane. Open your eyes."

"He will," Camilla said to Julianna, but she too had concern across her forehead. There were murmurs all around them as vampires resurrected in complete and utter confusion. Witches were explaining the situation and why their memories were murky. And still, Shane lay lifeless.

"Everyone has risen except Shane." Henna walked over to Julianna and Camilla, standing over Shane's body. "Is everything all right?"

Camilla smoothed his blond curls from his forehead. "His potion was a bit different than the others. But give him time."

Julianna tensed with concern. "Different how?"

Camilla's eyes never left Shane's face. "As unique as he is."

"What did you do to my brother?"

But just as the panic started rising in Julianna, Shane's arm twitched.

"He's awakening!" Henna shouted to the crowd, who gathered around Shane's body as it reanimated to life. His arms and legs started convulsing and he rose two feet from the ground between Julianna and Camilla as he writhed in whatever was taking place inside his body. His head tossed this way and that, twisting violently. His arms and legs continued to shake and twitch. It was like a mini-earthquake was going on inside of him. And then it stopped and he fell to the ground.

And he opened his eyes.

Camilla smiled openly. She hadn't lied when she'd said she'd stay by his side no matter what he chose, but she had to admit to feeling a sense of relief at the result. And Julianna gasped audibly before the tears fell from her cheeks and she threw her arms around her brother. Her now-human-again brother.

Shane sat up and hugged his sister firmly. And when she pulled away, she wiped her tears, although more kept coming, and then she began to explain what was happening just as she'd done for the others. She imagined he was confused and the memories were fuzzy and twisted inside his brain.

But Shane looked her in her eyes and grabbed her arms to stop her. "I remember everything, Jules."

Julianna looked at Camilla, who shrugged but was still smiling from ear to ear. *A potion as unique as he is.* Shane reached over and kissed Camilla quickly before standing up and taking stock of the scene all around him. He looked from face to face, searching. From them he saw all the confusion and fear that he had expected to feel, but instead he felt normal. Like nothing had happened. And yet something had.

His muscles were no longer super strong. He couldn't smell every scent in a five-mile radius. His eyes had difficulty adjusting to the darkness that enveloped them. He was human. No doubt about it. And yet he was a little surprised. He hadn't even known himself that that was what he'd choose.

And all around him, he saw human faces. "Did no one choose to remain a vampire?"

"I was a vampire?" a shocked Regina responded, clutching her bosom in horror.

But it was Isabelle who gathered her wits, and anger, quickly enough to accuse Camilla. "You did this to us!" And on instinct she ran at Camilla, arms fully extended. Her claws were gone now, but if she'd still had them, they'd be ready to tear Camilla's flesh from her bones. Shane ran to Camilla, in his feeble human attempt to protect her. But Camilla had never needed his protection then and she certainly didn't need it now. She flicked her wrist and Isabelle's soft human form spun across the grassy clearing and landed with a thud. And then she didn't move.

"Sorry," Camilla said. "I forgot she wasn't a vampire anymore." With another twist of her wrist,

Camilla let Isabelle get up slowly, clutching her middle and limping back to the gathering of witches and former vampires.

She glared daggers at Camilla. "You tricked us. You turned us all back into humans to defeat your mortal enemies."

Camilla shook her head. "No, I gave you a choice."

"Why should we trust you?" Isabelle spat.

"I wanted to be human again." It was Elias who spoke, his neck held high on his tall frame. He appeared less formidable but not less fierce in his human form. He still looked like a mighty warrior. "I'm tired of hiding in the shadows."

"I'm tired too," Luke announced. "I just want to be normal again. The normal life that was stolen from me. I want it back."

Shane walked over to Isabelle and took her hand gently. "Are you sure there isn't the tiniest part of you that wanted to be human again?"

Isabelle looked at Kara, who clung to Emily

with frightened tears rolling down her cheeks. Kara had been her protégé, and now she was just a girl. A scared little girl. What was Isabelle? She had been a vicious vampire warrior. What was she now?

She turned her attention back to Shane. He had been the most powerful of them all, and yet here he stood before her, just a man. Barely a man even. They were all just ordinary people. What did it all mean? "I guess…I guess I'm tired too. I don't want to be a monster anymore."

And she was completely embarrassed when her human emotions overcame her and a tear fell from her cheek. She hadn't cried in decades. She hadn't felt all these emotions in a very long time. And weirdly, it felt right.

"So, what happens now, Shane?" Luke stepped toward his best friend. His hair fell gently into his eyes. He was still as handsome as ever, just a little softer now. And Julianna thought she'd never seen anything more beautiful. "What was the vision if we stopped the prophecy?"

Shane walked back to the gathering, tugging Isabelle with him and placing an arm around Camilla. "We didn't stop the prophecy. We've begun eradicating vampires, just as was foretold. Everything Beatrice predicted has come to pass or is starting to. I just realize now that I misinterpreted my vision. It wasn't a disease; it was our choice. We all *chose* to be human again like Julianna."

At the mention of her name, Luke turned to her, like he'd suddenly remembered how much he loved her—and maybe that was true as his human brain slowly regained its memories. He swept Julianna into an embrace that lifted her off her feet.

"Everyone is welcome at the Strashni compound until you've fully recovered your memories. And then you are free to choose whatever human life calls to you," Shane announced.

"What about all the others? The vampires who didn't come to the clearing tonight?" Johann asked

Shane exchanged a look with Camilla before answering. "We'll send potions to everyone. They can all have the same choice we did."

"So that's it? We're all just starting over as humans?" Isabelle asked, her voice soft and hard to hear with their now human hearing.

But Julianna, still with one arm around Luke, told the group, "No one has to do this alone. There are potions to help you regain your memories, for those who want that. And as you decide how you want to live, we'll all be there to make it happen."

"I think I'll enlist," Elias stated, no waiver to his voice. "I'm a soldier and I need to have something to fight for. And now I can fight in the light of day."

"That's good, Elias," Shane encouraged, hoping others might also share their dreams.

"I'm going to find me a rich husband," Regina smiled ruefully. When all eyes turned to her, she added, "What? I've always wanted to be a socialite. And I don't remember everything clearly, but I know I won't make it living on the streets."

"I'm sure you'll find someone wonderful, Regina." Shane smiled at her, true to herself to the end.

"Johann?"

Johann cleared his throat, his face growing red, overwhelmed by all these newfound human emotions. "Many centuries ago, I was a lawyer, I believe. The memories are a little hazy, but I remember arguing in a court. I think I'd like to see if I can make that go in today's age."

"Can we continue this conversation somewhere else?" Luke rubbed his arms. "I haven't felt cold in a long time and I don't like it."

Julianna smiled up at the handsome man at her side. "Welcome to being a human."

"I forgot about things like being uncomfortable," Luke frowned.

Shane smiled, and the happiness met his eyes. Camilla realized that true happiness had eluded Shane his entire brief vampire existence. He'd battled vampires, witches, prophecies. Never a moment's rest. But now he seemed truly happy, listening to his friend's dreams. And she knew wholeheartedly that he would do everything in his power to help their dreams come true. Because that was Shane. Vampire or human. Leader or not. Powers or no powers.

Shane turned to Camilla, all the weight of the Prophecy finally gone from his face. In the end, it had all come true exactly as the Dark Prophecy had predicted. A powerful vampire had been born, able to control the elements, who'd come and united the warring vampire tribes. Ended the Shadow Wars. And then the vampire curse was overturned and vampires started becoming human. Only it wasn't the end, as they'd feared. It was the beginning of a new life for all of them—the lives they'd sacrificed to be turned.

Somewhere in the distance, a wolf howled. Shane wondered if it might've been the wolf that had been howling the night he was reborn as a vampire in St. Mary's Cemetery. Like there was some creature out there who understood his plight and was there to announce his resurrection as a vampire, and then came back for the chance to announce his resurrection as a human.

Shane leaned into Camilla and kissed her

forehead, so many possibilities before them. But whatever path they chose, they'd choose it together. "Let's go home."

EPILOGUE: 5 YEARS LATER

"Unka Johann, watch me!" The little blonde boy rolled down the grassy hill, headfirst in a somersault, then stood to make sure Johann had watched the scene unfold.

"What a talent, little Marcus," Johann responded with a smile. Despite being centuries old, he was just now finally starting to get the slightest dusting of gray in his hair and crow's feet accenting his eyes. And he loved it. "One day perhaps you'll be as great as your father."

With a smile, Johann looked playfully at Shane, who watched his young son get up and run to his mother, a very pregnant Camilla.

"Any names picked out for the baby?" Johann asked, squinting in the sun. Five years later and he still never tired of feeling the sun on his face, even as it blinded his human eyes.

"I'd like to name her Beatrice," Shane stated,

arms folded across his chest.

"So, it's a girl then? You're sure?"

Shane smiled conspiratorially. "We have our methods of being sure." And Johann knew that to be true with the chosen one and a witch for the parents.

"Well, I can tell you one thing. Beatrice would have loved to have seen all of this come to pass. And she would've been very proud of you." Johann placed a solid hand on Shane's shoulder. "You actually remind me a lot of her, ya know."

"The power of sight?"

Johann nodded. "And compassion."

Camilla approached Johann and Shane with little Marcus in tow. "Glad you could join our Prophecy Day celebration."

"Thank you for inviting me." Johann smiled at the pretty witch, remembering the day he'd awoken with human eyes after centuries of thirsting for blood. It was worth celebrating the fifth anniversary of the time they'd all gotten their human lives back. And then he remembered seeing Julianna's face when he first resurrected and the peace it had given him. "Will Julianna be joining us?"

"Yeah, she and Luke are just finishing up in the fields." Shane pointed to the crops neatly lined up in rows that stretched across their land. "No matter how many farmhands we hire, she always insists on being hands-on."

"Well, farming always was her dream," Johann said, and he followed the young Walker family into their large, white farmhouse.

"No special girl in your life, Johann? Even with a successful law practice? I'd think the girls would be throwing themselves at you," Camilla smiled as she helped Marcus wash up from playing outside in the large farmhouse sink.

Johann smiled. "She's human. Her name is Faith. I didn't know how to explain to her about Prophecy Day, so I just told her I was visiting old friends. She knows nothing of my past, just thinks I'm a huge history buff."

"Unless you date a vampire-turned-human like

us, I don't think you'll find too many women who can understand your true story," Shane responded, thinking how lucky he was that Camilla knew everything about him, even the dark parts.

"Do you still keep in touch with any of the old tribes?" Johann asked Shane. Camilla handed a pasta salad to Shane and a basket of rolls to Johann, and they talked as they helped set the dining room table.

"I do. As you know only a small handful remained as vampires, and most of them have returned to Europe for what they believe to be a freer existence. But there is a small tribe here on the West Coast." Shane placed his dish on the table and then sat in one of the chairs. "They've agreed to my terms to keep the numbers of vampires small, so we don't accidentally repeat the territory battles that led to the Shadow Wars."

"Smart." Johann also sat down across from Shane. "They are lucky to still have you and your guidance."

"They'd be luckier to have yours." Shane

nodded to his old, wise friend.

"Perhaps I took this second-lease-on-life thing a bit too seriously, but I needed a fresh start." Johann shook his head at the thought. "There's not much room for vampires in my new human life."

"Johann!" Kara squealed as she entered the room and saw the old familiar face. She was a young lady now, filled out and grown up in ways she never would have seen if she'd stayed a vampire. It warmed Johann's heart to see her moving past the frozen point in time her vampirism had locked her into. She ran to him, he stood, and she threw her arms around his neck.

"You look absolutely radiant," Johann beamed. And then he saw Emily waltz in, with their father, Richard, hard on her heels. "You all do. So great to see you all." He hugged Emily and shook Richard's hand. "Decided to live the farm life too, huh?"

"We tried to go back to the Ventura house, but there were just too many memories. It never felt right," Richard explained.

"So we sold the house and Camilla and I went

into business together," Emily smiled. "My dad does all our bookkeeping."

Camilla joined them in the dining room and began loading her young son in a highchair at the end of the table. "We are midwives and healers for the locals. As you can imagine, our results are miraculous." Camilla smiled, the cunning little smile that had earned her the nickname the poisonous flower.

"Well, if you are using witchcraft to help people, I won't judge," Johann answered.

"Camilla was just too talented to waste her powers on crops," Shane explained as he kissed her forehead and ruffled the hair of his young, curly blonde son. Emily cleared her throat, and then he added, "And Emily. She's gotten really good too."

"Is it time for the celebration?" Julianna walked in wearing dirty coveralls and thick mud-splattered boots. At least, Johann hoped it was mud they were splattered with. He no longer had his super sense of smell to be sure of it. Behind her walked Luke, but in contrast he was spotless with not a hair out of place.

"Is Julianna doing all the work? How are you so clean?" Johann asked, laughing to himself at how some things just never changed, even if their very nature had.

Luke crinkled his nose. "I don't do cows."

Julianna smiled up at her handsome husband. "Luke is more of a supervisor than a roll-up-your-sleeves kinda guy."

"I'm surprised you didn't head to Hollywood with that million-dollar smile," Johann said.

"Nah, never really appealed to me to be in the pictures."

"Movies, honey. No one has called them pictures in a century," Julianna laughed at Luke. "Don't eat until we get cleaned up." She grabbed Luke by the hand and headed out the way she'd come in.

"They live in the house on the right. Emily, Richard and Kara in the house on the left," Shane explained to Johann. "And I wouldn't want it any other way. Once you find a family, you don't want to lose it."

Johann nodded. How well he knew that to be true. He thought back to the vampire tribes. Sure, there was lots of fighting and vampire drama, but they had all been extremely close. Despite no biological connection, his tribe had been his family. And then with Shane, all vampires had become one large family. And as someone who'd lost his sister at fifteen, Johann assumed Shane was all the more desirous of keeping what connections he could.

"And what about Regina? And Isabelle? Have you heard from them?" Johann asked as they all sat at the table, waiting for Julianna and Luke to return so they could begin their Prophecy Day feast.

Shane looked at Camilla and they shared a small laugh. "Ah, Regina. I think she's eloping soon with husband number three."

"Three?" Johann asked, shocked. "In five years?"

"You know Regina."

Johann nodded with a smile. He did. Likely husbands number one and two didn't truly appreciate

Regina's boys on the side.

"And Isabelle and Elias both went into the military, but she rose through the ranks quite quickly and she now works for the CIA. She tells me it's a desk job, but I've never bought it." Shane smirked and then glanced at Camilla. They'd always been able to communicate without any words and, in that regard, it seemed like not much had changed even if his body had.

Camilla said something to Shane with her eyes and then turned to Johann and added, "Isabelle and Elias visit at least once a year. Sometimes more. Isabelle may finally get the respect she deserves."

"She's the reason I'm going to be getting my degree in Criminal Justice in the fall," Kara said with a smile. She had always looked up to Isabelle. It was no wonder that she wanted to follow her to Langley.

"And you, my young one, do you ever regret Prophecy Day?" Johann asked her directly.

She spared a glance at her sister and father before answering. It was clear that this topic had come up amongst them a few times. "No. Although I *was* a really amazing vampire…"

"You really were," Shane agreed.

"Like Isabelle I'm going to use the best of what I learned then and become an even better human. And I'm not perpetually a teenager." She shuddered dramatically at the thought.

As if he agreed, Marcus started fussing in his seat. Camilla started to get up to get him, but Emily was faster. She gestured to Camilla, "I've got him." And she picked him up, bouncing him on her hip like any good aunt would do.

Looking around the table, Johann asked a question that he himself had wrestled with since his turning back. "How do you protect yourselves without your powers? Is it all witchcraft?" Johann himself had tried to learn to fire a gun, but it had felt too awkward and noisy in his hand. Some days he found himself longing again for the ability to rip someone limb from limb with his bare hands. Especially at times in the courtroom, as much as he might hate it. Some old habits died hard.

Shane looked from Camilla to Emily, then to Kara and Richard. They were all smiling conspiratorially. So Johann had to ask, "What?"

Shane wiped his palms on his pants and then turned directly to Johann with his hand facing up. And then a fireball appeared. Shane smiled as he tossed the fireball back and forth between his hands.

Johann's eyes widened as he realized that Shane had been able to keep this gift. He had naturally assumed it had left him when he'd turned back to being a human. "You can still control fire."

"I can still control everything." To accentuate his point, he raised the lemonade out of the pitcher in one giant ball of yellowy liquid above their table. Marcus squealed and clapped his hands.

"Stop showing off," Luke announced as he again entered the room. Shane let the liquid fall back into the pitcher.

"But how?" Johann asked. "How is this possible?"

Shane looked at Camilla, who shrugged as if she didn't really care what the secret was. As if that wasn't what truly made Shane Shane. *A potion as unique as he is.* "Just lucky I guess."

"Don't bother, Johann." Julianna grabbed the seat closest to their ex-vampire lawyer friend. "We've been trying to get Camilla to admit it for five years. She never budges."

"But for a small fee, we *can* send you off with a potion that will slow your aging," Emily said with a wink, ever the saleswoman. She sat again with little Marcus on her lap.

"No, thank you. I meant it that night in the clearing when I said I was tired. I'm ready to grow old, believe it or not. I look forward to it," Johann said.

Shane reached for the dish in front of him, served himself and then passed it to Johann. It was nice to be sharing a meal with human friends that wasn't some derivative of human blood. Just good ole fashioned barbecue.

"I know exactly how you feel," Luke responded

as he passed the potatoes. "Also, it really isn't fair to average Joes that we look this good for centuries."

"As if you don't take the potion, Luke," Julianna said, rolling her eyes. Camilla just smiled at her family. She was good with secrets. She never would out who was taking what, so all she could do was smile at Julianna's playfulness.

When everyone had filled their plates with food, Shane raised his glass in the air with his hand. But after everyone had followed suit and raised their own glasses, he let his glass float out of his hand and stay hovering over the entire table.

"To second chances," Shane announced.

"To second chances," they all repeated.

And they toasted and celebrated the fulfillment of the Dark Prophecy—words that had at one time filled them with anguish and fear. Words that had foretold of an ending they had been afraid to face. A dark tale of Shadow Wars, unique powers, and the end of everything they had known. But in reality it was just a story of a boy who loved his family. A boy who used his power to guide them all to an ending, but who showed them there was no need to fear the end, despite his own initial misgivings.

Endings lead to new beginnings.

And they could rise again from the ashes and be strong. They could start again with a new life. And they would do it all together.

THE END

www.ingramcontent.com/pod-product-compliance
Lightning Source LLC
Chambersburg PA
CBHW030817210726
48290CB00002B/636